Cadell, Elizabeth
Mrs. Westerby Changes
Course

4.

Date Due			
Jan 31 '68	Jul 9 '68		
Feb 1 '68	Jul 13 '68	Aug 28 '70	Apr 13 '73
Feb 17 '68	Jul 31 '68	Oct 21 '70	Jul 31 '73
Mar 13 '68	Aug 23 '68	Mar 31 '71	Oct 17 73
Apr 4 '68	Sep 12 '68	Jun 11 '71	Jun 19 '74
Apr 11 '68	Mar 7 69	Aug 24 '71	Jun 26 '74
Apr 24 '68	Sep 9 '69	Sep 13 '71	Aug 7 '74
May 8 '68	Mar 2 '70	Mar 7 '72	Aug 23 '74
May 17 '68	Mar 23 '70	Apr 7 '72	Mar 21 '75
Jun 3 '68	Apr 6 '70	Apr 24 '72	Jul 24 '75
Jun 25 '68	Apr 13 '70	May 7 '72	Oct 10 '75
Jul 5 '68	Jul 30 '70	Mar 26 73	Oct 29 '75

Mrs. Westerby Changes Course

By the same author

THE CORNER SHOP
THE FOX FROM HIS LAIR
CANARY YELLOW
COME BE MY GUEST
THE TOY SWORD
HONEY FOR TEA
SIX IMPOSSIBLE THINGS
THE YELLOW BRICK ROAD
SHADOWS ON THE WATER
I LOVE A LASS
THE LARK SHALL SING
MONEY TO BURN
THE CUCKOO IN SPRING
AROUND THE RUGGED ROCK
ENTER MRS. BELCHAMBER
SUN IN THE MORNING
IRIS IN WINTER
LAST STRAW FOR HARRIET

Mrs. Westerby
Changes Course

by ELIZABETH CADELL

WILLIAM MORROW & COMPANY, INC.
New York 1968

Library of Congress Catalog Card Number 68-12146

Mrs. Westerby Changes Course

Chapter One

In winter, the view from the London office windows was not inviting. In the distance could be seen a stretch of the Thames, its banks lined with cranes. In the foreground were smog-blackened buildings, their roofs thrusting out ugly chimney stacks and small, dirt-encrusted dormer windows.

In the forest of brick and cement, only two trees survived; these grew in front of a gaunt, ugly building occupied by the century-old publishing firm of Beetham Brothers. When the wintry winds blew, the branches, like gnarled fingers, tapped incessantly on the window of old Mr. Walter Beetham's room on the third floor, and every February it brought him to the point of ordering the trees lopped. But his policy was to ponder well before taking any action; he was still pondering when spring came and muffled the tapping, tormenting fingers in gloves of tender green. Soon the hideous offices on the other side of the street were screened by leaf-laden branches; the cranes vanished, and only a glimpse of water was left, shimmering in the sunshine. The Beetham Brothers could now look out, if they wished, on a view that was almost rural. Countrified Miss Teller shouted to her employer, Mr. Harold Beetham, early in

May, in her twenty-eighth annual attempt to pierce through his deafness—and through his blindness to anything but the work on his desk. "Look—rustic! Bucolic!" she shrilled, pointing to the window. But Mr. Harold merely told her irritably that if she was feeling unwell, she might as well go home.

Instead of going home, Miss Teller took her exasperation to the room in which Miss Sinclair worked.

"He's eighty-four," she said, banging the door and speaking without preamble, "and Mr. Walter's only two years younger. I don't know how much longer I can go on shouting."

Abigail Sinclair's eyes, large and grey and black-lashed, rested sympathetically on her colleague, but in their depths was the gleam of humour that the Beetham Brothers—and particularly Mr. Thomas—found so disconcerting.

"Deaf-aids?" she suggested.

"Mr. Harold won't use them, and Mr. Walter sticks to his trumpet. You ought to know that by now—you've been here nearly a year."

"Over a year," corrected Abigail, and looked at Miss Teller's beanpole figure and long, thin nose and scraped-back hair and admitted to herself that the months had slipped by more quickly than she would have believed. Soon, she mused, she would be stuck fast, passed from one generation in the firm to the next, as Miss Teller had been.

She found herself recalling the day she had come for an interview. The Jamaican lift-man had pressed the button of the third floor.

"Mr. Harold, Mr. Walter, Mr. Frank, Mr. Thomas, Mr. Christopher or Mr. Adrian?" he enquired in one breath, rolling his eyes.

"I've no idea. The agency just said the Beetham Brothers."

"They's not brothers—not all of 'em. Only some of 'em. You come after a job?"

"Yes."

She was to have been interviewed by Mr. Thomas Beetham, who was in need of a secretary—but he, together with the other senior members of the firm, had been engulfed by the prevailing wave of influenza, and so Miss Teller had conducted the interview. She had engaged the candidate, and Mr. Thomas, returning to the office on his recovery, rang his bell and found himself gazing incredulously across his table at a figure he labelled—instantly and erroneously— Chelsea Set. From her smooth, fair hair to her long, lovely legs she looked like a symbol of modern youth—and a girl wearing tomorrow's skirt in his office was, to Mr. Thomas, as outrageous as a man wearing yesterday's stubble.

Her expression did nothing to reassure him. Instead of the modest, even cringing manner he had come to expect in the newly-engaged employee, he encountered a survey steadier and cooler than his own. His eyes fell to the figures Miss Teller had laid before him: twenty-four years old. No girl of twenty-four should be able to summon, in these circumstances, so much poise.

The girl withdrew; Mr. Thomas, ringing agitatedly for Miss Teller, was left with an impression of a rather square face with little or no makeup; a small nose, a humourous mouth and large, wide-set, extremely intelligent eyes.

Miss Teller explained her lapse in a manner fluent, firm and well-rehearsed. She agreed that Miss Sinclair was not the usual office type—that is, not the usual type for this office, but if Mr. Thomas would raise his eyes from his newspaper on his way to and from work, he would see a procession of Miss Sinclairs proceeding to and from their places of employment. No, Miss Sinclair had not stayed long in any job—but her employers had in every case been sorry to part with her. She did not add that the female staff of Beetham Brothers stayed so long with the firm because they belonged to a generation taught to link long service with success—and she did not think he would be interested in the fact that Miss Sinclair's clothes made the other women in the office look like extras in an Edwardian revival. Nor did she think it worth while mentioning Miss Sinclair's illustrious connections; Mr. Thomas was not a snob, though he sometimes found it useful to act like one.

Miss Sinclair had stayed, and Mr. Thomas had been unable to find any fault with her work—but he had never lost his initial disapproval. There was a touch of flippancy in her manner which seemed to suggest that there was a wide, wonderful world outside which had no connection with publishers—an idea Mr. Thomas found unsettling.

"It's time the old ones went," Miss Teller was saying gloomily. "But they won't. They'll hold out until they're carried out."

She spoke in jerks, and very fast, as if anxious not to waste her employers' time.

"Perhaps it's tactless to call their attention to the signs of spring," Gail suggested.

"I daresay." Miss Teller's nose gave the twitch it seemed to perform without its owner's cooperation. "But those trees . . . they're beautiful at this time of year. The view only looks like this in May. By July, the leaves are all bedraggled by petrol fumes, and by August, they're curling up ready to drop. Now's the one chance of getting to see the colour of spring."

Adrian Beetham, the newest and youngest member of the firm, came into the room and, catching Miss Teller's last words, glanced at her curiously; spring and Miss Teller seemed to him a grotesque combination.

"Getting fever?" he asked her lightly.

Miss Teller, taller by three inches, looked down her nose at him.

"If by that you mean to imply that I'm too old for spring fever, you're quite right," she snapped. "I shall be only too happy to remove my old bones from this office just as soon as you can persuade your grandfather and your great-uncle to remove theirs."

The door closed behind her with a crash, and Adrian walked to the filing cabinet and pulled out a drawer.

"Teller's touchy this morning, isn't she?" he commented.

Gail thought that Miss Teller's touchiness was less remarkable than her ability, after twenty-eight years with the Beetham Brothers, to quicken at each reappearance of the tender green leaves. She wondered if she would one day grow dry and waspish; time did strange things. The dapper Adrian might grow like his stout and pompous father, Mr. Frank, and already there were signs that Christopher Beetham, today so brisk and so efficient, was becoming a hidebound old fusspot like *his* father, Mr. Thomas.

"Life"—Adrian agreed with her unspoken thoughts—"is most peculiar, but could you brood over it some other time? I can't find the Stratton file."

"Your cousin took it."

"Christopher? What the devil for? I thought the social side of Stratton was my job."

"He said something about sales figures. Mr. Thomas had been asking."

"Then he should ask you, and not Christopher. All Christopher comes in here for is to look at you—for which I don't blame him—but I wish you'd keep him away from my files."

"I will. I promise I will. Now will you go away? I'm busy. What did you want Mrs. Stratton's file for?"

"Shall I go away, as requested, or shall I tell you, as requested?"

"Whichever you like. I suppose you want to fix this reception?"

"I do. How am I supposed to organize it if nobody lets me find out when, and where, and how many?"

"I think Mr. Harold wanted to decide when and where."

"Harold! My God! That means we can shelve the matter until next Christmas. I suppose he knows that Mrs. Stratton is talking about going abroad? This book's got to be launched before she goes."

" 'Launched' is good," Gail commented drily.

"Eh? Oh yes, I follow you. You mean the ship's well out to sea—serial rights, film rights, book-of-the-year I daresay, and so on and so on. Doesn't that make things difficult enongh without having Christopher and Thomas and Harold poking about? And this reception is—"

"I've just remembered. Miss Teller said Mrs. Stratton had agreed not to go abroad until after the reception."

"So Teller's in on it, too? That's splendid. Such a help."

"Don't get peevish."

"I am keeping my temper remarkably well. I am, after all,

the one who's supposed to be pulling this thing together."

"Why not Christopher?" she asked. "He discovered Mrs. Stratton, didn't he?"

Astonishment widened his eyes and diminished his air of sophistication.

"Is that all you know about it?" he asked.

"How much more is there?"

"How. . . . Oh well, I was aware that you gave the Beetham Brothers only a fraction of your time and interest," he said with heavy sarcasm, "but I should have thought that even you would have heard how we came by the book. Christopher must have told you the story."

"Well, Christopher didn't."

"Then I will. It came about—"

"Look," Gail broke in, "I don't have to worry about how you get hold of books, or why you're publishing them. My job is to keep behind Mr. Thomas, and that's full-time. My sole concern with authors is to fend them off until somebody's ready to deal with them."

"Mrs. Stratton's different. She—"

"She's certainly different. She's good-looking, she dresses well and she doesn't think she's a genius. Compare that with some of the other female writers we get in here."

"That alone ought to have roused your interest," Adrian pointed out.

"Why? I knew she'd gone from poor widow to rich author in three straight sets. I'm not paid to find out how she did it. That's your job."

"Couldn't you call it keeping a finger on the office pulse?"

"That's Miss Teller's job. Now will you go away and let me work?" She looked up at Christopher Beetham, who had entered the room. "Is that the Stratton file you're nursing?"

"Yes. Want it?"

"Adrian wants it."

Christopher handed it over.

"You've got to deal with the invitations," he told Gail.

"I thought that was coming," Gail spoke resignedly. "Got the list?"

"It's in the file. It's to be at the Courtier."

Gail made no comment. It was the most exclusive restaurant used by the Brothers, but for Mrs. Stratton, she knew, they were pulling out all the stops.

The two men went out; the door closed and then opened again and Christopher took a step into the room.

"Fixed the dates for your trip yet?" he asked.

"Yes," Gail said. "June the eighth."

"If you're driving, and you leave on the eighth, you can't possibly get to—"

"I'm booked on the car ferry to Bordeaux. I get off there and drive the rest of the way—which isn't far."

"What date are you meeting your brother at San Sebastian?"

"Ninth, I hope. Tenth if I'm delayed."

He hesitated before putting his next question. Like all the Beethams, he had found her impossible to classify. In his experience of women, which was considerable, that serene air in unmarried girls over twenty-three invariably pointed to a nicely-balanced sex life—but this girl had thrown his theories out of gear. Her flat was always swarming with her brother's naval friends; her sister was married to an ex-naval Commander and their farm in Sussex was a home-from-home for his still-serving comrades. Her circle was almost entirely male, but as far as he could discover, they all got the same treatment—cool and friendly. Not too friendly and somewhat too cool.

"I'll be around San Sebastian in the middle of June," he said. "I suppose the car wouldn't take an extra passenger?"

"That question," Gail told him, "has been put to me several times a day, over this telephone as well as the one in my flat, ever since I agreed to drive Tim's car out to Spain to meet him. They all identify themselves as his girl friends, but they're not the same as the ones he left here two years ago, which puzzles me. I don't see how he could have made all those new contacts from the quarterdeck of a frigate cruising in Far Eastern waters."

"What they call naval operations, I suppose. Well, I'm sorry I can't make one of the party." He glanced out at the mild sunshine. "It's beginning to look like holiday weather. All the same, I'd better get some work done. Which reminds me that your boss wants to see his list of luncheon fixtures. Take it into him, will you?"

Her boss was his father. She picked up the large black book in which the engagements were written, and made her way to Mr. Thomas's room, sensing, as she walked through the main office, the quickening in tempo that had been brought about by the spectacular success of Mrs. Stratton's novel.

It was a success unparalleled in the firm's annals. The resulting volume of publicity had produced in the Beetham Brothers a variety of emotions, but dismay was uppermost; they had a feeling of having been rocketed to the top of the pops, a position they had no wish to occupy. They prided themselves on having maintained, for over a hundred years, a steady and well-deserved profit from authors who, while producing nothing sensational, had an appreciative and faithful following. They were gratified by Mrs. Stratton's success, but they would have been more gratified had it been more moderate.

Her modesty and composure had won the admiration of all the Brothers. She had followed all the advice they gave her. She had surrendered herself to the literary agent recommended by Mr. Walter. She had earned Mr. Thomas's gratitude by her avoidance of what he called the more vulgar aspects of publicity.

He looked up as Gail entered, and gave his usual nervous cough. His room was large, but dark; the light from its single window was reduced by heavy curtains chosen by Mrs. Thomas, who as the senior surviving wife felt herself entitled to choose the office décor. Her more unfortunate mistakes were relegated by Miss Teller to Mr. Thomas's room; he had the bottle-green rug, the Beethoven bust and the plastic chrysanthemums. On a shelf stood a vessel that Miss Teller referred to as the unguentarium.

"You wanted to ask about your appointments, Mr. Thomas?"

"Ha. Yes. Yes, Miss Sinclair. Yes, yes. Thursday was what I had in mind. Thursday. What did I have on for Thursday? That's to say, this coming Thursday. Thursday of this week."

"You're lunching with Miss van der Ryls."

"Ha. No. You must do something about that. Mr. Harold, perhaps. I can't do it. I've got Mrs. Stratton coming to see me. Very important I should be free to lunch with her. See Mr. Harold, will you?"

"Yes, Mr. Thomas. The same restaurant?"

"Dear me, no. No, no, no," said Mr. Thomas, horrified. "Telephone to Alberto."

"Yes, Mr. Thomas."

Miss van der Ryls was a durable old lady who wrote animal stories for the under-tens. Gail unloaded her on to Mr. Harold, who was not pleased, but who understood the importance of leaving Mr. Thomas free to entertain Mrs. Stratton. Going back to her room and picking up the phone to speak to Alberto, Gail wondered idly how much of Mrs. Stratton's success with all the Brothers was due to her book, and how much to her gentle femininity and soft brown eyes.

"Neither," Miss Teller said, when she put the question. "It's just her manner. Quiet. Ladylike. What the Brothers like is the way she sits without fidgeting, and listens to them without interrupting. Very unusual in authors. The Brothers can't get used to it. I can see why people can't believe she wrote the book all by herself—but I never doubted it myself. Did you?"

"I haven't read it."

"You haven't. . . ." Astonishment choked Miss Teller. "Not *read* it?" she demanded, when she had sufficiently recovered.

"No."

"But you must! In the way of duty, for a start. It's. . . . Look, you take a copy home tonight. Read it."

"I've got no time to read during the week."

"Once you open it, you'll make time."

"You liked it?"

"Of course I didn't like it," Miss Teller snapped. "It isn't a book you can *like*. It frightens you."

"Thriller?"

"No, no, *no*. Didn't you even read the reviews?"

"No."

"Then take the book home and read it. It's nothing to do with thrills. It's simply a story about an old woman of eighty—written by herself, written about her life."

"What frightened you?"

"You'll find out. The theme is waste—wasted lives. Lives thrown away, like the old woman's. Long, dreary procession, cradle to grave—no joys, no tragedies, no nothing. That's the point—nothing. She lives what they call an exemplary life, and when it's over, she realizes that it didn't get her anywhere. She looks back and sees what she started out with —and what she ended with. All her early hopes, all her early promise, gone for nothing. Read it. Talking about it doesn't convey its . . . its *force*. Wasted opportunities, wasted time, wasted chances . . . that's why it's called *The Desert*. Leaves a peculiar taste in your mouth—you wonder who first said that virtue was its own reward—and why. It's a strong book. It's too strong, and that's why some people say that the husband must have had a hand in it. But I don't think so. They shouldn't be misled by her shy manner and quiet voice. She could have written it. Do you follow me?"

"You've just sold a book. You might as well go on from there and tell me how the Beetham Brothers got hold of it."

"Don't you know that either?"

"No. Don't bring up that fingers-on-the-office-pulse business; Adrian went into that."

"It's a complicated story."

"Tell me and see if I can follow."

Miss Teller looked across the desk with a frown.

"Considering the fact that you work for Mr. Thomas, who—"

"End of prologue," Gail broke in. "Just give me the fascinating facts."

"Very well. The doctor who treated Mrs. Stratton's husband happened to meet Christopher one evening in October, at the house of a friend. The doctor, who seems to be a bumbling but kind-hearted old fellow, learned that Christopher was one of the publishing Beethams, and got him in a corner and told him that the wife of one of his patients down in Cornwall had written a book—which he'd read. He said it was remarkable, it was extraordinary, it was . . . in short, might he, if the lady gave him permission, show it to Christopher?"

"So far no complications. The lady gave the bumbling doctor permission?"

"Yes. He said she'd written the book in the intervals of nursing her sick, probably dying husband. It sounded like a—"

"Buildup. But Christopher read the book?"

"No, he didn't. He put the thing aside. The next thing he knew—this was at the end of December—was that the husband had died. The doctor came to tell him. He asked what Christopher had thought of the book. Christopher couldn't tell him, because—"

"He hadn't read it."

"Worse. He'd lost it."

Miss Teller paused, halted by this astounding recollection.

"Lost it?" Gail repeated, her interest for the first time roused.

"Completely. He didn't find it for some time—and when he did unearth it, he read it unwillingly, because he'd got a picture fixed in his mind of a poor little woman scribbling down a novel in between bouts of nursing—"

"But being alert enough to bring it to the doctor's notice and ask him if he knew anybody who knew anybody. . . ."

"No, not quite. He just thought it would be infinitely pathetic, and practically unreadable. When he *had* read it, he was certain she couldn't have written it alone—but he'd got to know the doctor pretty well, and he was prepared to take his word. The doctor said the husband couldn't possibly have had a hand in it, physically or, in his opinion, intellectually. She wrote it alone. When she first came to the office, I was sure she could have written it; behind that mild exterior of hers, you get flashes of . . ." she considered, frowning, "of power, I think the word is."

"It's an elegant exterior," Gail remarked. "How old is she?"

"Thirty-eight. The husband was about twenty years older. Pity he didn't last until the money started to roll in. The doctor said they were pretty hard up towards the end."

"His widow's worth something now," Gail said, and picked up the telephone, which had been ringing for some time.

The voice that answered her own was so loud, so commanding, that for a moment she was swept back to her schooldays and had an absurd impulse to rise smartly to her feet. The look on her face made Miss Teller pick up the second telephone.

"That is the secretary of one of the partners, is it not?"

the voice roared in enquiry. "May I know your name, please?"

"Sinclair. May I—"

"You have a charming voice, Miss Sinclair. It is Miss, is it not? You sound so very young. Yes, I thought so. Miss Sinclair, my name is Mrs. Westerby. W.e.s.t.e.r.b.y. Westerby. I am extremely sorry to trouble you in this way, but I have been talking to my sister-in-law, Mrs. Stratton, and I understand from her that a reception is being given in her honour."

"Well, I—" Gail signalled with her eyebrows for help, but Miss Teller appeared too fascinated to heed her. "The invitations are—"

"Not out yet. So I understood. And so I thought that I would telephone to somebody connected with the Beetham Brothers and ask if my name and address might be taken down."

"Will you wait one moment, please?" Gail put her hand over the mouthpiece and made signs to Miss Teller: *"Can she come?"*

"What's to stop her?" Miss Teller signalled in reply.

"Are you there?" enquired Mrs. Westerby. "Oh, there you are. The name is . . . I've told you, of course. Mrs. Stratton wasn't quite sure about the formalities, so I told her that I would find out for myself if there was any possible objection to a relation of hers being included. I am her late husband's sister. You don't think there would be any fear of my being thought an *intruder?* Do speak frankly, please. You mustn't have the slightest hesitation in telling me if outsiders are barred. I call myself an outsider as a figure of speech, of course. I think I can claim with truth to be Mrs.

Stratton's nearest relative. But you have only to say the word and I shall withdraw."

Gail, her ears buzzing, sought in vain for the word.

"One moment, please," she said at last. "The senior partner's secretary is here. Miss Teller, would there be any objection to our sending an invitation to—"

"None that I know of," Miss Teller said into her telephone.

"Was that Miss Teller? Oh, good, good. I was almost certain that it was all right, but I do like to make sure, don't you know? Would you mind taking down my address, Miss Sinclair? It is Vizcaya Lodge. V.i.z.c.a.y.a. That's another way of writing Biscay—the Bay, you know? Vizcaya Lodge, Shern, Sussex. You have that down? Viz . . . Oh, good. May I apologize," roared Mrs. Westerby, "for having taken up your time with this small matter? Will you by any chance be at the reception? Yes? I am so glad. I shall look forward to meeting you there. Goodbye. Thank you, and goodbye. Goodbye."

Gail put down the receiver and drew a long breath.

"No need for deaf aids there," Miss Teller remarked. "Getting on for seventy, I'd say. Probably horsey. Hunted like mad in her day. Runs the village—Shern's a village, isn't it?"

"Yes."

"Isn't it near your brother-in-law's farm?"

"About eight miles away."

"Rather troublesome as a sister-in-law," Miss Teller mused.

"If Mrs. Stratton had wanted her to come," Gail asked

uneasily, "wouldn't she have said so? D'you suppose this loudmouth is just elbowing her way in?"

"Two hundred people, remember—and weather permitting, in the open. With luck, she'll lose herself in the crowd."

"Shall I mention it to Mr. Thomas?"

"Certainly not. Anticipating trouble. Don't worry," Miss Teller advised. "Mrs. Westerby can't hurt anybody."

Later—much later—it was this scene and this remark that were to recur most vividly to Gail. She was to recall how, incredibly, Miss Teller had asserted that Mrs. Westerby could do nobody any harm.

Chapter Two

GAIL spent the following weekend with her sister and brother-in-law at their farm in Sussex.

Her sister had married Alan Weekes, who had served for some years in the Royal Navy. He had met Noelle Sinclair at the time when he, with a great many others in his age group, fell under the demobilization axe; when he married, he had no job and very little money. As if to justify his faith in a beneficent Providence, an uncle died, leaving him two hundred neglected acres and a farmhouse. He and Noelle moved in. While Alan took his first cautious steps among the cows, Noelle inspected the dilapidated old house and proceeded to tailor it to her needs. By removing the wall between the kitchen and an adjoining room, she created a large, open-space living room; the other rooms on the ground floor were used as bedrooms and the dairy was turned into a bathroom. The empty, echoing upper floor was left to guests who brought their own sleeping bags and spread them out on the bare boards.

The household was run on haphazard lines, but the two children—a boy and a girl—were looked after by a treasure named Totsy. A relic of uncertain status, she had stayed on at the farm after the late owner's death—sole reminder of his somewhat libertine past, which had scandalized the district.

Gail always enjoyed her visits; lack of money, sagging roofs, straying cows, poor crops and high prices were accepted by Alan and Noelle as part of an impecunious farmer's lot; the compensations were an open-air life, Totsy and an unending succession of naval visitors. Christopher Beetham had not exaggerated when he classified the farm as a port of call. The once-elegant, once-slim Noelle was plump, and dressed in muddy slacks and shabby sweaters; Alan noticed no difference, and knew only that she was as pretty and as warm and as loving as ever.

She met Gail on Friday evening as usual, at the local station; conversation between them went on where it had left off.

"All set for San Sebastian?" she asked, as Gail threw her suitcase into the back of the station wagon.

"More or less. Getting the car papers is hell; I wish the thing wasn't in Tim's name. How's Alan?"

"Just the same." It sounded like a purr of content. "He's heard of a job for you, if you want it—secretary to the Naval Ski Club at Murren this winter. Interested?"

"You mean leave the Beetham Brothers?"

"Why not? You're due for a move."

"I'll think about it. The children all right?"

"Yes. And guess what—there's probably a little sister or brother on the way."

Gail turned to stare at her.

"Already?"

"Rebecca's two-and-a-half. Robert's nearly four."

"You said you wanted a pair. You got a pair."

"Alan says we've got to look ahead; many hands make light labour."

"Did he specify how many hands?"

"No. But there's a lot of room for more children."

"What about paying for their education?"

"Oh"—Noelle dismissed the problem with a wave of her hand—"we can think of that later. Heard from Tim?"

"Yes. He's sailing up from Gib with those Spanish friends of his."

"I daresay he'll marry one of those girls. But I hope not."

Gail removed her gaze from the farmhouse, which was coming into view.

"Why d'you hope not?"

"Well . . . I had an idea about him."

"So did I. But it's no use. He wouldn't look at her, and you know it. I hope you didn't raise Alan's hopes."

"I didn't say a word—but she's his only sister, and she's over twenty and not a soul has ever looked twice at her—out of all the dozens she's met here. Alan's wondering what's missing."

"He only has to sniff, to know. It was all right at fifteen to go round smelling of horse, but no man wants to—"

"I thought we might do something—you and I."

"Do what, for instance?"

"Well . . . get her out of those ghastly old jodhpurs of Alan's, for a start. And then take her to a decent boutique and rig her out, and make her go to a hairdresser. She might surprise us."

"I doubt it. Go ahead and try."

"You'd have to help," Noelle said. "You're not afraid of

speaking out, and you could bawl at her whenever she biffs a man on the back and knocks the breath out of him. It's that awful heartiness that does it—puts them off, I mean."

She brought the car to a halt in the yard. Two small human forms appeared from behind the disused pump, and Gail fended them off with her suitcase.

"No mud yet," she warned. "Wait till I change."

They led her to their room, where a camp bed had been put up for her; it was uncomfortable, but it was better than a sleeping bag on a hard floor upstairs.

"Pwesents?" Rebecca enquired hopefully.

"Don't ask, don't ask, don't ASK!" Robert yelled at her in panic. "You have to *wait*."

"Quite right," Gail said. "Never forget the old rule: Those who ask, don't get; those who don't ask, don't want." She opened her case and produced two small, gay pencil cases. "Here. One each."

"No guns?" Robert's face fell.

"Your father says no guns yet."

Alan, entering, confirmed this prohibition.

"No toy guns," he said. "Going pop-pop-pop doesn't teach you anything. I'll draw pictures for you with those lovely new pencils. —How's things?" he asked, kissing the cheek Gail presented.

"Fine. What's this about yet another mud-caked child?"

Alan smiled, his gaze on the fields to be seen from both the windows.

"Such a wonderful life for them," he pointed out. "Seems a shame not to produce 'em and let 'em enjoy it. Come and have a drink."

"You mean you've got time to drink? No cows calving?"

"Only Noelle." He picked up his daughter and led the way to the living room. "Now let's look at you," he said to Gail.

Studying her as he mixed the drinks, he thought she looked as good as usual, and was struck, as always, by the great likeness—and the great difference—between her and his wife. Both were good-looking, both easy and unaffected and good company—and after that, the differences began to show. Noelle was far more pliant, less intelligent, and as a wife, completely undemanding; she accepted him as he was and shrugged off his faults. He thought that Gail's husband—when she made up her mind to choose one—would be kept up to standard. And perhaps that was a good thing; a man needed a jab now and then.

"How's the job?" he asked. "Did Noelle tell you—"

"You'd got one lined up for me? That would only be temporary."

"You'd get some good skiing. While we're on the subject of jobs, isn't it time you chucked this office racket and got yourself a husband and some children?"

"Yes," Gail admitted. "It is."

"Then . . . ? You've only got to pull a string and you'll find a man at the end of it."

She leaned back in her chair and let Robert clamber on to her knee, speaking lazily over his blond head.

"It would be nice if I could fall in love," she said. "Really in love, as I did when I was seventeen. That was before your time, but Noelle can tell you. I was in a daze for months."

"Yes, I heard. And went to sea and came back two years later and you'd got over it."

"Yes. But it was wonderful while it lasted. I've never felt the same way since."

"You probably never will again. That was purely biological. The next time might not feel as good, but if you're lucky, it'll last." He took her glass and refilled it. "Odd to be talking like this," he said.

"It's odd to be talking at all. This is the first time I've seen you and Noelle alone for . . . oh, I can't remember when. Where's all the weekend crowd?"

"On the way."

"Doesn't Totsy ever complain?"

"What's Totsy got to complain about? They bring food, they cook it, they wash up, they take the kids off her hands and they do all the odd jobs. Ah, it's a bit late to point it out, but Robert's pants are making your slacks muddy."

"They'll wash." She stretched luxuriously and Robert slid to the floor. "Oh gosh, it's heaven to get away from streets and buses and dreary old publishers."

"How's your jackpot author?"

"Mrs. Stratton? There's a sort of party for her on Friday. Have you read her book?"

"Don't be silly. If I can open the *Farmer and Stockbreeder*, I'm doing well. If your publishers are getting you down, why don't you move? Did Noelle mention—"

"The ski job? Yes."

"It's yours if you want it."

"So I gathered."

"Why not take it on? It's much more your line than an office full of octogenarians with ear trumpets. Or perhaps," he probed, "there's someone younger there who's making things more interesting."

"There isn't."

"Then shake off the dust. Give your mind to marriage. Get out and take a look round. Find yourself a superman.

Nothing like ski slopes for separating the sheep from the goats."

"On the slopes, I'd settle for the goats. Robert, go and find Mummy and tell her we're drinking."

Robert went away, and Gail was about to ask Alan whether he knew or had heard of a peculiar old lady called Westerby who lived at Shern, when Noelle came in with the first two weekend guests, and the matter passed from her mind. From now until Sunday evening, she knew, the house would ring with male voices; heavy footsteps would tramp up and down the uncarpeted stairs and informal groups would gather round the great open fireplace. Gail did not wonder that the house never lost its appeal; besides the easy hospitality of Alan and Noelle, she knew that to enter the door was to see a home-at-a-glance. Every department of domesticity was open to view: sink, stove, ironing board, sewing machine, toy cupboard, television, record player, a long refectory table flanked by benches, and deep, comfortable, shabby sofas and chairs. Home at a glance, and while the visitors were in it, a real home; the kind into which, it was hoped, Tim Sinclair would be welcomed when he was in distant parts of the world.

Warm hospitality—but hardly a restful weekend, Gail acknowledged each Monday morning when she returned to the Beetham Brothers. Staying at her flat, however, would have meant as much or more company, for it was open to friends who wanted to be in town. Nevertheless, before this weekend was over, she wished that she had stayed at home, for pressure built up steadily to induce her to accept the job at Murren. She refused to give a definite answer, but she knew that she was ready for change and in the mood to con-

sider new possibilities. She made no promises—but in the
suitcase she took back to town were two pairs of ski pants
which no longer stretched sufficiently to encase Noelle's
plump thighs.

The atmosphere in the office on Monday morning seemed
to her more somnolent than she could bear. She thought
longingly of Switzerland, and snow, and ski runs. The
creaky old lift turned into a funicular; Mr. Walter's ear
trumpet assumed the size and shape of a Swiss cow horn.
It was only with an effort that she was able to bring her
mind to the work in hand—which included the prepara-
tions for Friday's reception.

She had sent out small, printed cards which stated merely
that the Brothers would welcome guests for drinks at the
Courtier Restaurant at half-past six. Her own part at this
and similar gatherings was a minor one, and confined to the
firm's family matters; Mrs. Thomas did not like Mr.
Thomas to have more than two glasses of champagne; Mr.
Frank was not to be allowed to slip away early; and Mr.
Harold's chauffeur was to appear at exactly fifteen minutes
to eight, to conduct him to his car, thus giving the signal
for the dispersal of the company.

Friday was fine and windless; the reception would be out
of doors. Miss Teller and Gail changed in the office and
drove in Christopher's car to Knightsbridge. The terrace behind the restaurant was spacious and screened; the sun
warmed the guests—all of whom Gail thought remarkably
dull.

"Well, we don't go in for the spectacular types," Miss
Teller pointed out. "And Mr. Walter won't have the teen-

age geniuses. Funny, isn't it, how the under-twenties have
taken over? They write the music, sing the songs, set the
ghastly fashions and rake in the profits."

"The old had a long inning," Gail commented lazily.

"Not long enough. I'm going to bring out a dictionary
of forgotten words," Miss Teller said, and ticked them off
on bony fingers: *mellow; delicacy; grace*. Now look at Mrs.
Stratton over there—there's delicacy for you. And grace.
You can't wonder she's a hit with the Brothers."

Gail looked at the slim figure walking beside Mr.
Thomas.

"I can never make out," she said reflectively, "how it is
that some people appear ready-made—spring out of nowhere into top billing."

"You mean she's been stuck in a house down in Cornwall, nursing a sick husband, and suddenly emerges looking
like this?"

"Yes. She's got a kind of old-world look, but that's only
her manner. Look at her clothes and her hair style."

Miss Teller looked. Certainly this was no gauche pro-
vincial hesitating at the entrance to the hall of fame. Mrs.
Stratton, for all her unassuming manner, carried herself
with a quiet assurance and dignity. But Gail, who by now
had read her book, found it difficult to link its tragic force
to the tranquil-looking woman listening so politely to Mr.
Thomas' platitudes.

"What did she do before—I mean when she was young?"
she asked Miss Teller.

"She went in for stage designing. That must have been
how she met her first husband, who was an actor. He had

a good deal of money, but he ran through it and died leaving her with nothing."

"And then?"

"Back to stage designing, and then Edward Stratton."

"How long was he ill?"

"Oh—months. Seven or eight months. They were only married for two years. Then she was a widow again."

"And then she was rich and famous."

"She deserves to be," Miss Teller said, and then dropped her voice and spoke in a warning tone. "We'd better try and look busy—old Mr. Thomas is staring at us."

Mr. Thomas was doing more than staring; he was approaching.

"Ha. Miss Sinclair. Will you come with me, please?" he said as he came up to Gail. "Mrs. Stratton would like to speak to you."

Slightly uneasy, Gail ran her mind over the last letter she had sent to Mrs. Stratton; there seemed nothing in it to warrant discussion. She took the gloved hand and heard Mrs. Stratton's slow, gentle voice.

"Miss Sinclair, I've been longing for a word with you. . . ."

She paused and smiled at Mr. Thomas. It took him some time to interpret the look, but the prolonged silence gave him a clue.

"Ha. Yes. If you'll excuse me," he mumbled, "I'll. . . ."

"Such a nice man," Mrs. Stratton murmured, gazing at his retreating form. "They're pets, all the Brothers." She waved a hand round the crowded terrace. "This is quite delightful." Her voice dropped to a confidential whisper. "That's the tenth time I've said that this evening."

Gail looked into the dark, amused eyes, and ceased to wonder at the homage offered by the Beetham Brothers. Charm, she acknowledged unreservedly. Charm—natural, effortless, not to be acquired or even imitated. A wave of liking rose in her and made her smile at the older woman.

"Doesn't counting make it more tiring?"

"Not so far," Mrs. Stratton said. "I do it as a kind of drill. It helps to make everything more real. How many people are there here?"

Gail told her.

"And all that tactful intermingling—I've been watching the Brothers. Do they do it by instinct, or habit, or is it all worked out beforehand?"

"Ask Mr. Thomas," Gail suggested smilingly.

"I will. He's been such a help to me all through these difficult months. He persuaded me that this party was, in a way, a family affair, and so I felt able to come."

It took Gail a moment to understand that this was a reference to the fact that Mrs. Stratton was still in mourning for her husband. That accounted, she realized, for Mrs. Stratton's choice of mauve for her beautiful suit—half-mourning. The word family brought something else to her mind.

"Your sister-in-law didn't come," she said.

Mrs. Stratton looked puzzled.

"My sister-in-law?"

"She was invited."

"I think perhaps you're mixing me up with someone else," Mrs. Stratton said. "I don't—"

"Mrs. Westerby."

There was a pause. A variety of expressions passed over

Mrs. Stratton's face, but Gail did not see pleasure among them.

"Mrs. Westerby was invited?"

"Yes. That is," Gail qualified, "she rang up and I spoke to her and she said she'd spoken to you and . . ."

"Ah." Mrs. Stratton nodded. "Yes, I see. It isn't quite true that she spoke to me about it, but . . ." She gave a slight shrug. "I ought to have realized that when she heard there was to be a reception, she would . . . I hope she wasn't troublesome?"

"Not at all. She just said she'd—"

"She just said she'd like to be invited. I'm surprised, if you sent her an invitation, not to see her here. I'd be grateful"—she gave Gail a fleeting, apologetic smile—"if next time, you'd get in touch with me before. . . ."

"Yes. I will," Gail promised.

"She means well," Mrs. Stratton said, "but she tends to— well, to follow me about. Nobody likes being followed about, especially by somebody as odd as Mrs. Westerby. And now"—She dismissed the topic—"may I come to my reason for asking Mr. Thomas to bring you to talk to me? I want to ask you a favour."

Gail waited. She wished that instead of chatting with Miss Teller, she had provided herself with something to eat and drink; the waiters were not circulating with anything like their initial energy, and she saw no hope of getting anything until Mrs. Stratton had set her free.

"I had a word with Miss Teller," Mrs. Stratton began, "and she happened to mention that you were driving to San Sebastian early in June."

"Week after next. Yes."

"May I ask if you're going alone? And if you are, is there the slightest chance that I could go with you?"

Surprise and dismay kept Gail silent. This was the last thing she had expected, the last thing she wanted: the company of a total stranger.

"I'm not going to San Sebastian," she heard Mrs. Stratton say. "I've got to get to a place, a house, on the French side of the Pyrenees, and it's almost impossible to get there by public transport. There isn't even a village. Before you say anything, I'd like to add that it wouldn't be far out of your way. If it were, I wouldn't dream of asking you to take me. But . . . are you going alone?"

"I'm going alone, but I'm not driving all the way. I'm booked on the car ferry from Southampton to Bordeaux."

"That's what Miss Teller said. From Bordeaux, it would only mean three or four hours' driving. I could fly out to Bordeaux and meet you off the ferry—if you would agree to take me, and if you would agree to letting me pay your expenses."

Gail hesitated.

"I don't—"

"Please let me explain," begged Mrs. Stratton. "I don't own a car, and I can't drive. I could of course hire a car and a chauffeur, but it would be so much better, so much nicer to be with someone like yourself. The place I'm going to is called Chandon. There's a hotel there, and I've got a room. The cottage I'm going out to see is just near by—actually on the hotel grounds. I promise it wouldn't be far out of your way, and if it meant staying a night at Chandon, I would book you a room at the hotel and I would ask Mr. Thomas to give you an extra day's holiday. Would you consider it?"

It seemed unreasonable to refuse to consider it. While Gail hesitated, Mrs. Stratton gave her more details.

"My husband left me the furniture that's in the cottage. The cottage itself belongs to his sister—the Mrs. Westerby you mentioned just now. The furniture is said to be valuable, so I want to look at it and make up my mind whether to bring it to England or sell it abroad. I should only ask you to take me there; don't be afraid that I shall want to be with you and your brother on the return trip."

Gail was not in the least afraid; she knew that Tim would have plans of his own, and they were not likely to include Mrs. Stratton.

She made some rapid calculations. She knew that Mrs. Thomas, under cover of joining a nearby group, had been listening to every word—but she was not worried about Mrs. Thomas or about the Brothers. Her holiday was her own business and she would not drive Mrs. Stratton unless it suited her to do so. But if it meant only a few hours' extra driving, and no extra expense, and if she could readjust her schedule slightly so as to meet Tim as arranged, she saw no objection to the plan. She said so, and saw Mrs. Stratton's face light up with relief and pleasure.

"My dear . . . I'm so grateful! I could hardly believe you would agree. I know I'm asking a lot. Look, I'm staying in London. May I ring you up and fix a day for lunch? Then we can make the final arrangements."

Gail was not surprised to see Mrs. Thomas joining them. After listening to Mrs. Stratton telling her what she had already overheard, she said graciously that an extra day's holiday could of course be arranged.

"Getting to Biarritz or Bayonne would have been easy enough," Mrs. Stratton said, "but feeling my way round the

Basses-Pyrenees, looking for an out-of-the-way cottage, would have been rather too much."

"Then that's all settled," Mrs. Thomas said with decision. "I shall speak to—"

She stopped abruptly, halted by a disturbance that seemed to be taking place at the long glass doors that led from the restaurant to the terrace.

"Who on earth," she said in amazement, "can that be?"

Gail knew. There could be no mistake. This was the owner of the voice that had bellowed at her over the telephone. She could only marvel at the accuracy of Miss Teller's sketch.

The woman who was dealing kindly but firmly with Miss Teller in the doorway was so enormous as to raise doubts of her having been able to pass through it. She was dressed in what Gail, gazing at her in fascination, decided must be the contents of a theatrical wardrobe. There was a short, jaunty Elizabethan page's cape over one shoulder; a Robin Hood's hat over grey, stringy hair; Oliver Cromwell's buckled shoes; and a dress—long and elaborate and high-necked —that could have been used on alternate nights by Lady Bracknell or Charley's Aunt.

But it was no figure of fun that put Miss Teller firmly to one side and advanced across the lawn. The hazel eyes, almost lost in encircling bags, were keen and shrewd. The cheeks were pendulous, the chins numerous and quivering, the mouth open and fishlike—but authority was to be read in every line of the figure as it steadily advanced with heavy tread.

"There's some mistake," Mrs. Thomas said loudly. "I shall speak to—"

She stopped abruptly. The newcomer was approaching Mrs. Stratton with arms opened wide and a face beaming with pleasure.

"My dearest Anita!" she bellowed, halting before her. "Do forgive me. I'm so sorry, so very, very sorry to have arrived so late. Or is it"—she turned to the frozen Mrs. Thomas—"is it your forgiveness I should be asking? You must be a Mrs. Beetham-Brother, must you not, since I understand this is purely family? Perhaps . . ." her gaze went round the keenly attentive assembly and lit unerringly on Mr. Thomas ". . . ah, yet another Brother? I am right? I thought so. I have a little gift, do you know? I can pin professions to people. I can say unhesitatingly, That Person"—she pointed directly at Mr. Harold, who shrank closer to his chauffeur—"That Person is a publisher. Correct again? I thought so. But I'm not going to show off. This is not my party. It is Anita's, is it not?"

No longer, thought Gail. Mrs. Stratton, who a few moments before had occupied the center of the stage, with becoming modesty, had faded into insignificance beside the huge, commanding figure of her sister-in-law. The reception had assumed an underwater character; small fish seemed to be swimming round a whale.

Gail withdrew to a secluded corner of the terrace, and Miss Teller joined her. From there it looked as though Mrs. Westerby's clothes had been put on over a series of loosely connected balloons. She was informing those about her that she was delighted to be there, delighted to be able to join in the congratulations and perhaps even in a measure share Mrs. Stratton—Anita's—triumph. Her voice filled the air; her gestures were unrestrained and theatrical.

"Off her head?" Gail asked Miss Teller in a low voice.

Miss Teller was looking puzzled.

"That's what I thought when she came in. But now. . . . No, I don't think she's off her head."

"Crazy or not, she's killed the party."

They looked across at Mrs. Stratton. Her face had not lost its composure; only a heightened colour told of her anger, or embarrassment, or both. Miss Teller's glance went back to Mrs. Westerby.

"I'm only guessing," she said, "but I'm willing to wager that she lives in a large house in a small village, and throws the garden open for sixpence a head when in bloom. In her spare time, she's British Legion, Women's Institute, Church Roof Restoration, Hospital Appeal, Unmarried Mothers, Anglo-American Unity and Anti-Litter."

"I still think she's crazy."

"That's because you're not old enough to recognize the type. They're dying off, but there were lots of them around once upon a time. They were the sort that used to baffle foreigners."

Mrs. Westerby, like royalty, was doing the rounds. The groups on the terrace, mesmerised, re-formed into a double line down which the large figure made its way, the deep voice filling the silence. She spoke graciously to established authors and encouragingly to the up-and-coming. She patted Christopher and Adrian on the shoulder and called them twigs of a fine old tree.

"Grotesque, but grande dame," summed up Miss Teller. "Mrs. Stratton's bearing up well, isn't she? But she can't like it. What did she want to talk to you about?"

"She's meeting me at Bordeaux and I'm driving her to a

house somewhere in the Basses-Pyrenees. On my way—I trust. I'm not quite clear where it is."

Almost immediately, Mrs. Westerby told her. She had come to the end of the lines and was peering across at Gail.

"Miss Sinclair? I thought so. I asked Mrs. Stratton to point out the young lady to whom I spoke on the telephone —and here you are. She told me that you are driving her to Chandon—how kind of you! No, Miss Sinclair, no more champagne, thank you, delicious though it is. I love good wine—it's the French side of me—did Mrs. Stratton tell you that my mother was French? She lived at Chandon before she married. Then the big house was sold and turned into a hotel, and my mother built a little cottage on the grounds —and that's where you're going with Mrs. Stratton. My brother and I kept the cottage on when my mother died. We had always spent our holidays there, and we both loved it. Mrs. Stratton has never seen it—she and my brother never went there. I am so glad you are going with her. I shall be going out at the same time and we have arranged to meet there."

Gail was so certain that this was a prelude to asking for a place in the car that she began to frame a resolute refusal —only to learn that Mrs. Westerby's travel arrangements were already made.

"I myself am driving out with my godson. We were only waiting to get a definite date from Anita—Mrs. Stratton. Do you know the Basque country?"

"Not very well."

"Spoilt, a good deal of it. Ravaged. When I was young, it was idyllic," roared Mrs. Westerby. "The cottage is rather out in the blue, so I hope you'll be able to find the way."

"I'm sure I shall," Gail said. "I've got a large-scale map and—"

"Plenty of good, sound sense—I can see that. Such a rare thing in a pretty girl. But those roads in the Basses-Pyrenees are very confusing. The Basque names confuse people, though I don't know why, really. You know, if you glance at a map of Scotland, you can see names every bit as tongue-twisting, like Sithean Mor and Sgurr an Utha and Fraoch-bheinn. I studied Gaelic for a time, you know—helped, I confess, by my father, who was a professor of languages."

"Not Oswald Stratton, by any extraordinary chance?" Mr. Frank put in from behind her.

Imagining this to be a rescue operation, Gail felt grateful—but a glance at Mr. Frank, as she made her escape, convinced her that the coincidence had made him beam with pleasure; he was listening with interest to Mrs. Westerby as she talked about her late father.

There was a stir at the other side of the terrace; Mrs. Stratton was leaving. The plan had been that Mr. Thomas and Mr. Frank together would act as escorts—but Mr. Frank was reliving his linguistic past, and Mr. Thomas was trying to explain to his wife that he had known nothing, positively nothing of any invitation to any Mrs. Westerby. It was Christopher Beetham who went to Mrs. Stratton's side, as representative of the firm.

"Anita, you're not leaving?" Mrs. Westerby shouted. "If you'd wait a little while, I could go with you. Perhaps we could have a little dinner somewhere?"

Mrs. Stratton did not shout back. Without pausing, she went away, and it had to be admitted that it was not the exit the Brothers had meant it to be.

"I do hope," said Mrs. Weserby, "that I'm not the last to go. If I'm enjoying myself, I tend to let time slip by. But I must be firm with myself. Goodbye, Mrs. . . . Thomas? Thank you so much! It's been charming. Goodbye, Mr. Thomas, goodbye. Lovely party, lovely. Mr. Frank, I can't tell you what a joy it has been to find someone who actually remembered my dear father. He died at ninety, hale and hearty to the end, like your delightful older brothers over there. How charming of you to have remembered him! Do allow me to send you a little paper he wrote—not for publication, no, no, no! It deals with the history of languages—that was his hobby, you know. May I send it to you? Or better still"—she turned her ungainly body, peering this way and that—"Oh, there she is! If you could persuade your nice Miss Sinclair to come out on Sunday and lunch with me, I would give her the paper and I could also show her exactly how to get Mrs. Stratton to our little cottage at Chandon. Miss Sinclair, do say you will! I don't live far out of London—but perhaps you spend your weekends in the country?"

"Miss Sinclair usually goes—am I right, Miss Sinclair?" asked Mr. Frank, "to stay with her sister in Sussex."

"What part of Sussex?" Mrs. Westerby enquired.

"A place called Downleigh," Gail told her, and heard a loud cry of astonishment.

"Downleigh! My dear girl, I live . . . but you know! I gave you my address! Shern is only eight miles from Downleigh! Do, I beg you, come over and lunch with me. I shall send my taxi to fetch you. What is the address?"

"Green Willow Farm."

"No! It isn't *POSSIBLE!*" roared Mrs. Westerby.

"You're not related to that young man who inherited it from Colonel Weekes?"

"He married my sister."

"Then you must, positively must, come and see me—and I must renew my acquaintance with your brother-in-law. He won't remember me, but I knew his naughty old uncle very well indeed. My goodness, he was a shocker! Do say you'll come! I shall give you the paper for Mr. Frank."

Gail decided to go. She did not like the look in Mrs. Thomas' eye; Mrs. Westerby had pushed herself in, had called Mrs. Thomas a Beetham-Brother, had made nonsense of the firm's smooth arrangements and wrecked the party. There was trouble coming, and it would be useful to have Mr. Frank as an ally.

"You're very kind," she told Mrs. Westerby. "But don't bother to send for me. I can—"

"Nonsense, nonsense, nonsense! I shall send my dear old driver. Let us say, Sunday, at a quarter to one—just us, and entirely informal. Mr. Frank, you will remind her?" She studied him anxiously. "You do, I take it, really want to see the little paper?"

She was assured by Mr. Frank that he wanted very much to read the little paper.

"Then that's settled. Sunday at a quarter to one, Miss Sinclair. I shall show you my garden—I'm very proud of it. Goodbye, goodbye. . . ."

Her exit was regal: a hand upraised in general salute, a kind smile for the company to share, Mr. Frank at her elbow, Mr. Walter behind as though drawn on an invisible string. The last roar died away; the guests faded away; the reception was over.

"I'll stay and support you," Miss Teller said, as Mrs. Thomas advanced. "After all, the invitation was as much my doing as yours."

"Next time—"

"Will be just the same, only next time, it'll be Mrs. Thomas issuing the invitations."

"She'll never let Mrs. Westerby in again," Gail asserted.

"Don't you believe it. What Mrs. Westerby wants, Mrs. Westerby gets. By hook or. . . ."

She paused, and Gail looked at her curiously.

"Or—?"

"Or by crook, I shouldn't wonder," Miss Teller ended, and prepared to put Mrs. Thomas in her place.

Chapter Three

On Saturday night, Gail went to a dance. She did not arrive at the farm until the early hours of Sunday. She slept late, and then went down to the orchard with her niece and nephew and a Shetland pony; the pony had the fun, the children the thrills, and Gail the exercise.

In a neighbouring field, Alan was mending a trough which had begun to leak. When he had finished, Gail walked with him to the house. A savoury smell floated out to greet them.

"Rosbif." Alan sniffed appreciatively. "Pity you won't be here to lunch."

Gail thought so too. The table was laid for nine, the joint was in the oven; one amateur cook was peering into saucepans while another peeled potatoes; a third was mixing salad in a vast wooden bowl.

"Can't you call this lunch of yours off?" Alan asked, opening a cupboard and beginning to mix drinks.

"No. I'm being called for."

"How far are you going?"

"Only to Shern," Gail said. "And that reminds me. Do you remember someone—"

Alan had turned, bottles in hand, and was staring at her in surprise.

"I didn't know you knew anybody at Shern," he said.

"I don't. I was just going to ask you about someone called Mrs. Westerby."

"Mrs. Westerby! What on earth . . ."

"You know her?"

"Everybody knows her. What are you going to see her about?"

"Some paper or other she's giving me for one of the Brothers."

"What connection does she have with publishers?"

"She's Mrs. Stratton's sister-in-law."

For some moments he was too amazed for speech.

"Well I'm . . . You mean that the Shern Strattons . . . you mean this author you've been talking about is the woman who married Edward Stratton of Shern?"

"She married an Edward Stratton. I didn't know he—"

"Why on earth didn't you tell me?"

"I didn't know he had any connection with anyone living near here. You've never once mentioned Shern, except to tell us that your uncle supported its pub single-handedly. How did I know there were any Strattons there?"

Noelle, folding garments on an ironing board in a far corner of the room, put in a word.

"Is Mrs. Westerby the enormous woman we ran into at that cattle sale last month?" she asked Alan.

"That's the one," Alan said. "Edward Stratton was her brother."

"You knew him?" Gail asked.

"I met him once or twice when I came down here to stay

with my uncle. I can't say I knew him—or that I remember him very well—I was only about eighteen. I heard later that he'd married a widow who lived somewhere in or near London, and—apart from a brief visit just after they were married—she and Stratton never came to Shern again."

"I don't wonder," Gail said. "How would you like to stay with Mrs. Westerby?"

"I shouldn't mind at all," Alan answered. "She's inclined to bellow, but she's amusing and she's no fool." He turned back to the cupboard, still murmuring his astonishment. "Edward Stratton's widow! Well, well!"

Totsy brought the children in, and nothing more was said about Shern or the Strattons—but when the taxi came for Gail, Mrs. Westerby was in it. Alan walked out to the decrepit vehicle and handed out the large figure seated inside.

"Mr. Weekes. I don't suppose you remember me," Mrs. Westerby said, standing and surveying him. "Do you retain your naval rank, and should I say Commander?"

"You can just say Alan. It's clever of you to recognize me after all these years."

"It isn't clever at all," Mrs. Westerby told him. "You look just like your uncle."

"God help me," Alan said simply.

"You look just as he used to look when he was your age," Mrs. Westerby amended, and turned to greet Noelle, who had come out of the house. "If this is your wife," she said, holding Noelle's hand warmly in her own, "you'll never suffer from loneliness and go to pieces as your poor uncle did. Has your sister-in-law told you I'm taking her off to lunch?"

Gail, finding eyes turned towards her, made an effort to

recover from the astonishment into which she had been plunged since Mrs. Westerby's arrival. She had been trying to connect this sensible, matter-of-fact woman, clad in a neat, dark suit and a small, smart hat, with the carnival figure that had disrupted Friday's reception. Mrs. Westerby had not shrunk, she was still outsize, her voice was still a trumpet blast—but there the resemblance ended. Gail wondered confusedly if the clothes in which she had appeared the other day had been Mrs. Westerby's notion of what the smart woman would wear to a London reception. The thought, however, only increased her bewilderment.

"Won't you come in and have a drink before you go?" Alan was asking.

Mrs. Westerby glanced through one of the long windows at the animated scene in the living room. Astonishment kept her silent for some time.

"Goodness gracious!" she said at last. "I wish your uncle could see that picture of hospitality. He shunned us all, you know—he wouldn't have any of us in his house. Did you knock down the wall between those two rooms?"

"Yes," Noelle said. "And we're all on one floor. Visitors go upstairs."

"One, two, three, four, five visitors," counted Mrs. Westerby, still gazing with undisguised interest through the window. "And such nice young men. Navy?"

"Most of them," Alan said. "They're no bother. They turn up with plenty to eat and drink—and as you see, they're useful about the house."

"They are indeed," Mrs. Westerby said, and reluctantly withdrew her gaze. "I feel very guilty, taking your sister-in-law away from you all. Are those your two delightful children in there?"

"Yes," Noelle said. "Don't be misled by the dirt. They start off clean every morning."

"How lovely, how lovely to be young and dirty," Mrs. Westerby said wistfully. "What a perfect place this is for children. Did you expect to inherit it? Everybody thought it would go to whichever woman happened to be living with your uncle at the end."

Alan laughed. "I didn't expect to get it," he said, "and if I hadn't had to leave the service, I wouldn't have been interested. As it was, it was a godsend. But I'm no farmer."

"Neither was your uncle—but he was a good judge of cows," Mrs. Westerby said. "And—though I wouldn't like to say so, except to you—a good judge of women. Every one of them was either a beauty, or a magnificent cook."

"And only one at a time," Alan said. "We inherited the last one."

"Totsy Baker? She was once my housemaid. Your uncle stole her. I'm afraid you didn't inherit much money—the Colonel was very generous to the ladyloves he pensioned off. Ah me, those were the days! And now, I must take Gail—may I call you Gail?—away with me."

Gail followed her into the taxi. The journey was a long, drawn-out affair, for the driver was as decrepit as his taxi; at every curve of the road, he slowed to a walking pace and played a fanfare on the horn. Gail would not have been surprised to see him get out and walk round the corner to see if anything was coming. They reached a little village at last, and entered a drive leading to a large, beautifully proportioned house.

"That's it," Mrs. Westerby said. "This was the house my

mother came to when she married. My brother and I were born in it. But I don't live in it now," she added unexpectedly. And Gail saw that the taxi, instead of drawing up at the entrance, was going round the side of the house and along a narrow, stony lane, to stop at last before a very small cottage with a thatched roof.

"Here we are," Mrs. Westerby said. "I moved here—it was the gardener's cottage—at the end of December—just after my brother died. I knew I should never need the big house again. It was a good idea, don't you think, to move into smaller quarters?"

It would have been, Gail thought, following her into the cottage and tripping over a chair and a footstool, if the move had been made without moving all the furniture too. It was impossible to believe that a woman as large as Mrs. Westerby could move at all in the room, crammed as it was with chairs, tables, chests, stools, pictures and china ornaments. Nothing, Gail felt certain, had been left behind at Vizcaya Lodge.

"It's not large," Mrs. Westerby pointed out unnecessarily. "At first, I must admit I felt a little cramped—but I soon got used to it. I felt—oh dear, I should have warned you that there was a little step there!—I felt I couldn't bear to part with any of my . . . no, it doesn't matter at all, it was my fault for putting so much china on that little table. Just come and sit here by the fire."

The fire was two logs set in a grate no larger than a frying pan. Mrs. Westerby removed the wire screen, rolled the logs into a new position and pushed aside two tables in order to allow Gail to draw nearer.

"If you own lovely things," she said, "—and all these are

lovely, don't you agree?—you can't, you simply can't make
up your mind which you're going to keep and which you're
going to part with. I ended by keeping most of my favourite pieces."

So much was evident, Gail thought, and tried to warm
her cold hands. It was all right for Mrs. Westerby to warm
herself at this one-candlepower heat; Mrs. Westerby had
several layers of natural protection and could have slid down
a glacier in comfort. Less well-cushioned guests were at a
distinct disadvantage.

"I expect you're wondering why I haven't got a little cat
or a dog to keep me company," Mrs. Westerby said. "The
fact is that I'm out of the house a good deal—committees
and so forth—and I hate leaving the poor things alone. Mrs.
Meredith, Julian's mother—Julian is my godson, and you'll
meet him presently, because I asked him to pick you up on
his way back to London today—his mother looks after his
three beautiful dogs, and would gladly keep an eye on mine,
if I had any, but I've decided against it.

"Besides, I'm worried about damage to my rose garden,
and my little vegetable garden, and my herb garden which
you can see through that side window. Put another log on
the fire, Gail—oh, I see the basket is empty. I can't remember whether I asked Julian to fill it for me or not. He does
these little things for me when he comes down to see his
parents at weekends. He works up in London. Computers.
His parents live down here and are my greatest friends. Just
push that knitting off that chair and sit down, won't you?
It's cosy in this little room, don't you think?"

"Very cosy," Gail agreed, and felt that Mrs. Westerby
would have got on well with her grandmother, who lived

in the few remaining habitable rooms of a crumbling castle
and said that draughts were healthy.

"My friends thought I wouldn't fit into this little house
—but as you see, I do," Mrs. Westerby said with satisfaction. "There were only two small rooms, two up and two
down. I added a little kitchen at the back, with a bathroom
above it, and here I am. I wouldn't have moved out of the
Lodge while my brother was alive; he was very fond of it,
although he only saw it once after he was married. We were
born in it, you know. I left it on my marriage, but came
back when I was widowed a year later. He never left it until
he married. Do you like drinking before lunching? I have
some sherry, if I can lay my hands on it. I asked Julian to
get me some and I think I put it . . . would you mind getting up for one second while I peer into that little cupboard
behind you? Can you see a bottle of sherry there?"

"No."

"That's very odd. We had a . . . Oh, now I remember!
I took it along to the church bazaar as a little contribution.
I'm so sorry. Could I make you some lemonade or some-
thing of that sort?"

"No, thank you."

"You haven't taken off your coat—let me have it, and
then you can settle down comfortably. That's right. And
now tell me how a pretty girl like you comes to be working
for all those dried-up old gentlemen."

"An agency sent me."

"I thought their reception the other day a little dull,"
Mrs. Westerby said. "Nobody seemed to stand out. Will
you come into the dining room and talk to me while I put
the mats on the table?"

She opened the door of the adjoining room. Gail, following her in, came to a halt on the threshold and the years fell away as she looked at the confusion of objects before her. She had seen them all before, in the crumbling castle: the sewing machine, so ancient that the makers would have been happy to put it on show; the thick red woollen mittens, the gardening gloves and battered straw gardening hat, the Chinese bowl spilling out snippets of material, the mangy fur foot warmer, the snuffboxes gaping with pins; pot-pourri; a rusty music stand; and a small bust of Wellington hung with skeins of wool and surmounted by a man's hat—the godson's, or the dead brother's?

She was aware that Mrs. Westerby was standing on the other side of the oval dining table and holding out a photograph in a large silver frame.

"This . . . this was my brother," she said.

Gail took the frame and saw a handsome, kind, rather weak face. She stared at it with a kind of wonder filling her mind; there had been so much of his widow in the fat files in the office, so much discussion, so many interviews. And after his widow, his sister had entered the scene, creating as much or more interest. But of the link between the two women—this man whose likeness she held in her hand—little or nothing had been heard. And nobody had been interested.

"He was a splendid-looking man," Mrs. Westerby said. "That doesn't do him justice. Everybody who met him, liked him. The photograph was taken just before he met Anita. He'd been staying with friends who had some connection with the theater. They gave a party, and she was there. Three weeks later, they were married." Mrs. Westerby took the frame and replaced it on the sideboard. "A thunderbolt."

There was a pause.

"Why?" Gail asked.

Mrs. Westerby, taking table mats out of a drawer, looked at her enquiringly.

"Why what?"

"Why a thunderbolt? I mean . . . men do marry, even men who leave it as late as your brother did."

"Yes, they do," Mrs. Westerby assented readily. "Of course they do. And in nine cases out of ten it turns out extremely well, as in my brother's case, except that he fell ill the year after they were married. She nursed him devotedly, and he was devoted to her. All the same, it was a risk—and for the people nearest to them, it's a shock. He and I had no close relations. I was an only child for twelve years, and then, to the astonishment of my parents, Edward appeared. As I told you, he and I lived at the Lodge all, or almost all, our lives. We didn't go to school and sometimes I think I must be the last child to have been educated by a governess. I was taught at home, and well taught. Edward had a tutor, as he was too delicate to be sent away. He—" She broke off. "Look, my dear Gail, you mustn't let me ramble on. You must be starving. We must eat. I hope you'll like what I've made for you. I don't claim to be a cook."

Gail followed her into the kitchen wishing very much that she had eaten something before leaving the farm. She had had no breakfast, and the cold weather had given her a wolfish appetite which she saw no prospect of satisfying. But when she stepped into the miniature kitchen, she saw with relief that it was really a kitchen and not a furniture warehouse. What was more, a savoury smell was issuing from the oven.

"The only thing I ever attempt," Mrs. Westerby said, putting on a voluminous apron and seizing an oven pad, "is a casserole. I simply chop up anything I can lay my hands on from the garden, add some meat or chicken or fish, cover it up, put it into a moderate oven, count seven thousand and take it out again. There!" She took off the lid of the casserole, sniffed, and nodded with satisfaction. "All right, I think. It's been in perhaps a little bit too long. Now follow me and make a good meal, as this is all I shall give you. Did I forget the mushrooms? No, there they are, the dear little things. Just find a chair somewhere, will you, and let me fill your plate."

It was even better than it looked and smelled—and it was also a treasure hunt, for Gail located not only mushrooms but leeks, tomatoes, red and green peppers, small cubes of chicken and veal, shreds of bacon, slivers of olive and thin slices of savoury sausage. The dish was deep and full at first, but as Gail dipped, and dipped again, Mrs. Westerby watched her with a face pink with gratification.

After lunch, two more logs were thrown onto the dying fire; by the reviving warmth, Gail sat cradling a large cup of coffee. Drowsily she recalled the purpose of her visit.

"Paper?" Mrs. Westerby looked blank. "What paper?"

"The paper you're giving me for Mr. Frank."

"Oh—that!" Mrs. Westerby waved airily. "Just remind me before you go. And now tell me about your brother—this brother you're going to meet in Spain."

"Navy."

"Did you say your grandmother brought you up?"

"Only after my parents died. She lives in Scotland, and we go up for holidays. My sister and my brother and I took a flat in London. Noelle doesn't use it now, and Tim's away a good deal, but I've kept it on."

"And he stays with you when he comes home?"

"Most of the time."

"You sound very united. So were we—Edward and I . . . that is, until he married. After that, I scarcely saw him."

Gail put a question with characteristic directness.

"Why didn't they come up here on visits?" she asked.

Mrs. Westerby stared at her as though the answer was to be found on her own face.

"They came once," she said slowly. "But only for a day—and never after that. Not once. I try to look back and reconstruct their visit, to find out what went wrong—because something did go wrong. I think perhaps it was myself. I know I'm a rather tiresome old woman, even an absurd old woman. I suppose she couldn't. . . ."

Gail wondered if, on that sole visit, Mrs. Westerby had appeared as she was today—sensible, likable, normal—or if she had arrayed herself in the collection of garments that she had worn at the Beetham Brothers' reception. If the latter, it was easy, remembering Mrs. Stratton's look of cold distaste, to imagine her dismay at the first sight of her sister-in-law.

"I thought at first," Mrs. Westerby was saying in the same slow, puzzled tone, "that Anita and I would have had a lot in common—particularly our love of beautiful furniture and ornaments. The day they came, I showed her round the house and she admired its contents very much—they are beautiful, you know, though perhaps you can't see them properly when they're all so crowded together. I sometimes wonder if she felt that the Lodge, and the land round it, and the furniture, should have been Edward's and not mine. She must have seen that they all had considerable value. But my parents left them to me—not only the Lodge, but also the little cottage near my mother's old home in France. Edward was left the bulk of the money as they thought that a fair division. The only furniture Edward got—and it's worth a great deal—is in the cottage in France, where my mother put her most cherished pieces. Anita is going out there to look them over."

"Didn't she ever go there when your brother was alive?"

"Never. You see, it was my cottage—as she kept reminding Edward when he mentioned it and suggested a visit. I realized that she felt deeply about . . . well, about property. I think she thought the division unjust. I made over a great many valuable pieces—miniatures and so on—to them when they married, but perhaps it would have been better to. . . . What does it matter, now? They never came again. And later, of course, Edward found travel tiring, and couldn't have stood the journey."

"Why was he delicate? I mean, did he have anything the matter with him specifically, or—"

"All his life, he was subject to terrible coughs. My parents always nursed his lungs. But it wasn't in the lungs, as it turned out, that the trouble lay. His stomach was the weakest part. It was that, in the end, that killed him, not his lungs."

Mrs. Westerby had carried her coffee cup to the window and was staring out into the wooded garden. She seemed to have forgotten Gail.

"I suggested making this house over to them," she said, "but Edward wouldn't hear of it. Neither would Anita. She said it was damp round here, and he would be better in the south. So they rented a cottage in Cornwall. I went down to visit them there—but they never came here again."

She turned to stare at Gail, but Gail knew that she was seeing something far away.

"A cottage in Cornwall can be charming," she said after a time. "That's how I imagined it—on a cliff, perhaps, overlooking the lovely tumbling sea. Or in a little village, the sort that artists paint. But it wasn't like that at all. It was a bleak house—not at all a cottage of the kind I'd imagined. It was at the end of a dismal little village, very windy and— I couldn't help thinking and saying—very damp. And also too big for them, but Anita said that the one thing Edward dreaded was having other people's things round them, and so they had brought their own furniture. There was quite a lot of it, and I could see it wouldn't have fitted into a little cottage, but I thought the whole place so . . . so *cheerless*. I begged them to come and live at the Lodge, and said I would live somewhere else—but Anita is very proud, and they wouldn't accept the offer. When I went to see them, I realized that money was getting short. Anita wouldn't take any from me, because she pointed out that my income, like Edward's, might dwindle to nothing. So there they were, in that comfortless house. I can see, now, how irritating I must have been—I used to suggest remedies that my mother had used when Edward was a boy—quite useless. I wanted them to go and live at the cottage in France, but Anita said that nothing would induce Edward to leave Dr. Belldon, who attended him—our own family doctor who had moved down to Cornwall for his wife's health. When

I spoke myself to Edward, he said Dr. Belldon was worth more than a Mediterranean climate."

There was silence—a prolonged silence, though Gail did not notice it. Edward Stratton seemed to have moved out of the shades and come forward to enable her to place him between the two women to whom he had belonged. It was almost possible to feel his presence, for so much in the room, she recognized now, was his. She had felt no interest in Mrs. Stratton and, before today, none in Mrs. Westerby, but her imagination was stirred by the picture of the trio— brother and sister and wife—which had become so clear while Mrs. Westerby spoke.

But Mrs. Westerby offered no more comments on the past. She took Gail round the herb garden and the rose garden; they made a leisurely tour of the empty rooms of Vizcaya Lodge. Returning to the cottage, she turned out the contents of two cupboards and three drawers before coming upon the map she was seeking; having located it, she spread it on a table and traced the route that Gail was to follow from Bordeaux.

"Some people might tell you to go down to Mont-de-Marsan—don't. Go to Langon, and from Langon to Pau. Here." Her fleshy forefinger stabbed it. "Are you following? Castres-Gironde, Podensac, Preignac—lovely sounds, aren't they? Now here you are at Langon. Now you make for the road to Pau—practically a straight line. You go, at first, through Les Landes. After a time, you'll get some magnificent views of the Pyrenees. Do not enter Pau. Forget about your map from this point, and let me give you this little sketch I've drawn for you. You see? You take this fork and begin to climb—rather steeply after a time. You're in the

Basses-Pyrenees, and ahead of you are the old smuggler's passes—but you won't be going as far as that. At this point here, you take the curve to the right, and soon you'll come to my mother's old house, which is now a hotel. The road goes on and skirts a little lake and brings you to the cottage. It's all quite, quite lovely and you won't regret having come out of your way to take Anita there." She folded up the map. "Have you made all your final arrangements with her?"

"I'm going to lunch with her at her hotel—the Flamingo —on Friday, to tie things up. Could I have the paper now? It's time I—"

"Paper?"

"The paper for Mr. Frank," Gail said, and was struck by the uncomfortable conviction that no such paper existed, or that if it did, it had no great importance and had been used merely as a means of getting her to the house. Yet the thought was so absurd that she could not entertain it for long. She watched drawers being pulled out once more, and their contents turned over.

"It should be in here, in this . . . no," Mrs. Westerby muttered. "I do so wish I had more room to keep things. I distinctly remember putting it—oh, come in, Julian," she called with obvious relief, as the door of the cottage opened. "Come in!"

Gail looked up to see the doorway almost filled by a man's large form; she saw with surprise that he was much younger than she had expected. She had been expecting someone middle-aged, but this man was only in his thirties.

He could not see her, as she had retreated behind a cupboard door to allow Mrs. Westerby more room for the paper hunt. He glanced round the room and spoke briefly.

"Hello, Blanche. I see that girl didn't turn up. Just as well. I'm in a hell of a hurry."

Gail came into view and spoke in a cool tone.

"I did turn up, but if you're in a hurry, you don't have to wait for me," she said.

"Oh—sorry. I didn't see you," he said in a tone far from contrite. "I'm having car trouble, so I'd be glad if we could get off at once."

"Of course, of course, of course," Mrs. Westerby assured him. "But wouldn't there be time even for a little cup of tea?"

"I'm afraid not, Blanche."

"That's a shame. This is my godson Julian Meredith, Gail. Julian, this is Gail Sinclair, who works for Anita's publishers."

He nodded, but did not relax his impatient attitude; Gail thought he looked like a horse pawing the ground. She felt that a friendly smile wouldn't have delayed him unduly, and found herself resenting his arrogant assumption that she would fling on her coat and dash out to his car, panting her gratitude for his condescension in stopping to pick her up.

"I'm waiting for a paper," she said. "Mrs. Westerby was just trying to find it."

He raised his eyebrows.

"If it's only a paper, surely it can be posted?" he suggested.

Gail wished she had proposed this sensible plan when Mrs. Westerby and Mr. Frank had approached her at the reception—but she was here, and this pawing horse would have to wait.

"The paper," she said, "is what I came here for. It's for someone in the office."

"If Blanche posts it tonight, it'll get to the office almost as soon as you will," Julian said. "But if you insist on waiting for it now, perhaps it would be as well if I went off and—"

"Wait! Wait a moment!" Mrs. Westerby cried. "I think I know where it is. One moment, Julian, one moment."

She went with hurried, shambling movements to a corner of the room and began to pull at a heavy chest that barred her way. Julian went to her assistance and dragged it aside, but irritation gave him a strength that sent the sharp edge against his shin. He said a word that made Mrs. Westerby gasp.

"Julian!"

"I'm sorry. The blasted thing's torn my trousers."

"It could happen to anyone," Gail said, and saw with satisfaction that they were very expensive trousers. It served him right for over-dressing on a Sunday. He was probably in a mad hurry to get back to town to take a girl out to dinner. No, not a girl; he was clearly one of those sophisticates who took mature and successful actresses to expensive restaurants and pretended not to notice when the photographers came and crouched beside the table. He ought to be in a shirt and jeans, using this nice day to do something active, like Alan. You wouldn't find Alan in a natty lounge suit on a Sunday afternoon straining to get back to stinking London and onto the nearest plush sofa.

"No, I was wrong," Mrs. Westerby said ruefully, standing ankle-deep in papers she had dropped in her search. "It isn't here."

"Let me pick those up," Gail said, crossing the room and dropping on her knees.

She handed the assortment of papers up very slowly, one by one, raising her eyebrows in contempt whenever Julian seized a handful and pushed them roughly into the nearest drawer.

"Could the paper be in that desk over there?" she asked Mrs. Westerby as she rose.

"It might," Mrs. Westerby said hopefully. "How kind and helpful you're being."

"I give you both exactly five minutes," Julian said. "After that, I'm afraid Miss Sinclair will have to make other arrangements for—"

"Don't be bad-tempered, Julian." Mrs. Westerby was pushing her way past obstacles, and at last reached the drop-front desk. She opened it, and a shower of documents fell to the floor.

"Let me," said Gail.

"Oh, thank you, Gail. Just push them in anyhow. I'll tidy it all later, when you've . . . got it!" she shouted in triumph. "Got it! Now do you see, Julian? It only needed a little patience. You don't find things by standing in the doorway and harrying everybody. If Gail hadn't been so—"

"Three minutes," he said. "Do we go, or don't we?"

Gail found her coat and he held it for her; not with so rude a jerk, she told herself resentfully, would he drape mink round the shoulders of all his sleek mistresses. She thanked Mrs. Westerby, took the paper and put it into her handbag, and then accompanied Julian to the car he had parked outside. Powerful and expensive, she noted—as was only to be expected—and plenty of room in the back for picnics.

They drove away, leaving Mrs. Westerby waving on the gravel. Julian said nothing; frowning, he listened anxiously to the engine and now and then tested the controls. Gail leaned back and conceded unwillingly that the cushions were superbly comfortable. Then she sat up with a jerk.

"That's not the way!" she exclaimed. "You should have taken that left-hand turning."

He slowed down and turned to look at her.

"I'm on the London road," he pointed out. "Or I will be once I get past—"

"But I'm not going back to town! I'm going to Downleigh."

He brought the car to a halt and looked at her with loathing.

"My godmother asked me to give you a lift back to town," he said. "That's what I'm doing—once I've called in at a garage to ask them to fix—"

"I don't care what your godmother told you," Gail said. "She came in a so-called car to fetch me from my brother-in-law's and knew I was going back there. All you've got to do is stop at a garage, as planned, and I'll arrange a lift from there to Downleigh, and thank you for all your kindness and courtesy, and let's agree that this is the last time I'll give you any trouble, and I hope your engine falls out just as soon as they fix it."

Without a word, he turned the car and drove back to the turning they had passed; soon they were on their way to Downleigh. There was complete silence for two miles.

"If I was impolite," he said in cold tones at mile three, "I apologize. But I was asked to call at my godmother's to pick up a girl who—I assumed, or my godmother told me— was going back to town. I've got a date there and I didn't want to miss it."

"She'll wait."

Silence fell once more. At mile six, she gave a brief direction.

"You don't go into Downleigh. The farm's on the Brender turning."

"I probably knew that long before you did," he said. "I used to ride over during school holidays and see old Colonel Weekes."

"I'm surprised your parents allowed you to."

"My parents thought it would broaden my outlook. It did. Not that I ever got inside the farmhouse. It wasn't exactly a haven of hospitality. Are you going back to town later tonight?"

"Yes."

This was the only exchange they troubled to make. Julian reached the farm gates, and as they were open, drove into the yard. Parked there were the farm station wagon, the children's cart and three dust-covered cars.

"I won't ask you to come in, as you're in a hurry," Gail said. "Thank you for the lift."

He had got out and opened the door on her side. The window of the living room was thrown open, and Noelle put out her head.

"Tea," she said. "And homemade scones. Come on in."

"He's in a hurry; he's got a date in town," Gail said. "Julian Meredith—my sister, Noelle. And her husband, Alan," she continued as the kitchen door opened. "And Commander Luke, Commander Godwing, Lieutenant Mount and Lieutenant Orr-Knowles—Tom, Jake, Chass and Carlo respectively."

"I made the scones, and they're magnificent," Jake claimed without modesty. "Gail, you missed a wonderful lunch."

"How come you go out with an old lady and return with a large packet of man?" Chass enquired.

"He picked me up. He's got to go. He's got a date—and car trouble."

"Bad luck about the date," Alan said, "but we've got three practically resident mechanics. Let's take a look."

One head, then two, then four bent over the engine. Gail walked into the house and poured herself out a cup of tea.

"What's the trouble?" Noelle asked, eyeing her moody expression. "Did he try anything on the way here?"

"He didn't even know I was female. I delayed him on his way to some peach-skinned beauty, and all he wanted to do was open the door and hurl me out. He's Mrs. Westerby's godson—maybe I forgot to mention it."

"He's very good-looking."

"He's yours. Where are the children?"

"Totsy took them out. They won't be long—not with the smell of those scones to draw them home. Do you think we'd better take tea out to those men? They'll be there hours, by the look of it."

She poured tea and took the cups out on a tray, and the men drank as they worked, picking up buttered scones in grease-blackened fingers and turning their attention once more to the job in hand. Gail washed up the tea things, poured milk for the children on their return, while Totsy got their bath ready; then she took over the ironing from Noelle to leave her free to prepare the supper.

She heard the men coming in when they had finished. They washed their hands at the tap outside and then streamed into the warm room.

"Don't be silly," Alan was saying to Julian as they entered. "The garage would have taken hours over the job. You've got time to meet the children—and also to have a drink before you go."

Gail watched Julian's entry. It was always interesting to note the reactions of strangers who expected to enter the normal drawing room or living room or kitchen. She saw him halt as his astonished eyes took in the scene: Totsy at the table with the children, herself at the ironing board, Noelle standing in the space between sink and stove. A bridge table was open in one corner; a model battleship was being built in another. Home-at-a-glance.

"No time for a rubber, I suppose?" Jake asked hopefully.

Julian, on the point of refusing, must have reflected that he owed something for the efficient repair made to his car.

"A short one," he said. "Could I make a phone call first?"

Telephoning was as public as everything else in that room. Julian picked up the receiver; Alan tactfully turned on the radio, but everybody could hear the shrill protests of someone called Mavis, who made it clear that she was not used to being Stood Up. Then Julian, his colour considerably deepened, took his place at the bridge table with the three, who had been making the best of things with three-handed games. The brief snatches of conversation between games seemed to run on computers. Gail went into the children's bedroom and began to get her things together.

"Lost him?" Noelle said, coming into the room.

"I'll live. I'm thinking of going back to town with him. The others won't want to leave until they've eaten, and there's a lot I could do if I went back early."

"Suit yourself. You'll be here again before you go out to meet Tim, won't you?"

"Yes," Gail said, and went out to speak to the bridge-players.

"If you can spare the new recruit," she said, "I'd like to go back to town with him. And not too late, either."

"You can't drag a chap away without a drink," protested Alan. "Besides, you'll miss Lydia."

No hardship, that, Gail mused. Lydia was his sister, and she would come in windblown, mud-covered and the conversation would be entirely horse.

"Here she is," she said gloomily.

Lydia entered and with difficulty prevented her horse from coming in too.

"Out, Hector, you brute!" she shouted. "Out! Hello, chaps. Guess what—I've bought a colt."

Julian, with the other men, had risen; he was staring at her in surprise.

"From us," he said. "I didn't connect you with—"

"Of course!" Lydia—tall, athletic and as strong as the horses she loved—took two strides and gave him a shattering slap on the back. "You must be Julian Meredith! I say, your mother's a marvel, isn't she?"

"She likes animals," Julian said cautiously.

"She knows more about horses than anyone I ever met," Lydia declared. "She stopped me from buying one from those swindlers over at Lowshern. Come on out and take a look at Hector."

"I'm. . . . Some other time," Julian said. "We're just finishing off this game, and then I've got to be off."

"Oh—bosh!" Lydia gave him a blow on the chest that made him stagger. "Off to where? Come out and see if you approve of the colt's new quarters."

"Go away and let's finish this game," Alan ordered. "And take Hector to the stables, where he belongs. Hector, get out!" he yelled.

Hector withdrew his head from the doorway and followed Lydia reluctantly to the stables. The men resumed their game, and at its end, Julian rose to go.

He and Gail had a good send-off; no man, she thought, had ever mellowed so much in so short a time.

"Where's the flat?" he asked as they reached the London road.

"Queen's Gate—one of those old houses converted. Two flats on each floor."

"Do you share?"

"Only with my brother. He pays half the rent, and in return, I entertain his friends."

"Male or female?"

"Both."

"I heard your sister talking about a job in Switzerland. Are you leaving the publishers?"

"I might. I've been there about a year. Over a year, in fact."

"You needn't apply at my office. We don't take transients. What's the point of training a girl to the point of usefulness and then seeing her melting away?"

"The agency doesn't mind how often I move—just as long as I do well in every job they put me in. I suppose you want your secretaries to grow long-service beards?"

He ignored this, and presently she asked where he lived.

"Just behind Harrods. I go down to Shern most weekends. I've got three dogs which I keep at home."

"This trip you're doing with Mrs. Westerby—is it your vacation, or just an extra?"

"A bit of both. My father thought she ought to have someone with her. In my opinion, she needn't make the trip at all. Mrs. Stratton could quite well have looked at the furniture by herself, instead of dragging Blanche out all that way just because she happens to own the cottage."

Something in his voice made her turn and look at him. "Don't you want to go?"

"No." The word came out with a force that surprised her.

"Did you get talked into taking her?"

"Yes." He spoke reluctantly. "That's about how it was."

"Do you know Mrs. Stratton?"

"No. I knew Edward—her husband—all my life, of course. I think he was meant to be my godfather, but there was always this feeling that he was going to die young—so Blanche became my godmother instead."

"Did he work at anything? Mr. Stratton, I mean."

"No. He didn't have to earn a living—he had a good income, though he lost most of his money later. He used to paint a bit—rather smudgy landscapes. He exhibited now and then at a small gallery in London."

"Did you like him?"

"Everybody liked him—he was a nice chap. Pity he left Blanche in the lurch after he married. But one can understand that, too. Do you like her, or do you find her odd?"

"Both." She paused. "You didn't like getting caught up at the farm just now, did you?"

He hesitated.

"I don't feel at home with service people," he said at last. "Not your brother-in-law's age group, anyway."

"Alan's thirty-two. How old are you?"

"Only two years more than that, but service people make me feel senile. Perhaps it's because they're all full of what's called boyish charm—or because they talk a language outsiders can't follow. Does your sister have a crowd like that every weekend?"

"Yes. They don't make any work—you saw them helping."

"It isn't my idea of a nice, quiet weekend."

"So I saw."

He frowned.

"You shouldn't ask questions," he said, "if you're not going to like the answers."

"That's true. I hope all your future weekends will be nice and quiet."

"Do you ever do anything about keeping that temper of yours in check? Would you like to stop for a drink, or would you prefer to go straight to your flat?"

"Straight to the flat, please."

He took her there and carried her suitcase to the lift and watched her go up, and went away feeling that he had not been at his best. His mind went back to the farm, and he found himself smiling as he remembered Lydia and Hector, and the children rosy from their bath, and Noelle rolling pastry for an apple tart.

And then he remembered his godmother, and the smile faded, and all pleasant thoughts drained out of his mind.

Chapter Four

FRIDAY'S lunch with Mrs. Stratton was not at all like visiting Mrs. Westerby and dipping into a steaming casserole.

The address on Mrs. Stratton's letterhead read, simply, FLAMINGO HOTEL, LONDON, W.1. The simplicity was misleading. The hotel embraced not only the expensive block of flats to the left, but also the building on the right in which a variety of amenities—sauna baths, shops, banks, beauty salons and a swimming pool—were available to residents; thus ensuring that there was no need for them to give themselves the trouble of setting foot outside.

Mrs. Stratton's apartment was on the eighth floor. Gail was conducted to it by way of a beautifully appointed reception room, a long, blue-carpeted corridor and a lift with cushioned seats. She could not decide whether the tall, smiling young porter, the tall, smiling young receptionist or the tall, smiling young liftman deserved the highest marks for suavity and elegance. In the end she decided that the accolade must go to the tall, smiling young gentleman who took over from the liftman, and who appeared to own all the suites on the eighth floor.

He led her toward a door on which was written—in silvery letters—Eight-Seventeen. He pressed a bell, waited to hear Mrs. Stratton's invitation to enter, ushered Gail inside and withdrew.

"How nice to see you." Mrs. Stratton held out a hand and smiled in welcome. "Please come in."

Gail entered, sent a swift glance round the room and decided that this was the sunny side of fame, the garland round the neck of the champion, the rosette on the winning horse. This was where you could put your feet up and say you'd arrived—though not for long, if you'd arrived at the Flamingo—she knew that even a success like *The Desert* couldn't pay the Flamingo fees forever. There would have to be more books, which meant work—and this was not a working atmosphere. Far from. This charming drawing room bright with chintz and bowls full of roses was designed for leisure.

"It's pretty"—Mrs. Stratton led Gail into the bedroom, took her bag and gloves and laid them on the brocaded bedspread—"and it's comfortable too. It's almost cozy."

Gail thought it was about as cozy as a Stately Home on public view day, and was surprised that Mrs. Stratton had done so little to offset the half-a-crown-entrance look; there were few books to be seen, no personal touches and not a single photograph. Chintz and brocade and flowers notwithstanding, the place struck her as devoid of life.

They walked slowly back to the drawing room.

"Drink?"

"Please."

"Will you help yourself—and me too, please. I'd like some sherry." Mrs. Stratton took the glass Gail brought her.

"You look so nice," she said. "I think you must love beautiful clothes as much as I do."

"I'm what they call a clever shopper," Gail said. "I get to the boutiques just as they're unpacking the new stuff. It's a useful instinct."

She took the chair her hostess indicated, and wondered how much Mrs. Stratton's suit had cost. Still lilac, she noted; still half-mourning.

"Have you," Mrs. Stratton asked, "thought very carefully about taking me on as a passenger? It's not too late to withdraw, you know."

"I'll enjoy having you," said Gail, and almost meant it. There was something about Mrs. Stratton that appealed to her; as she had tried to explain to Miss Teller, she admired the ease and swiftness with which Mrs. Stratton, after being shut up so long with a sick husband and very little money, had adjusted herself to fame and prosperity.

Mrs. Stratton was looking round the room; she gave a shrug, half-apologetic, half-amused.

"It's rather overdone, of course," she said, "but I'm enjoying it all so much. . . . I can't explain how much. You see, in a rather childish way I'm trying to make up to myself for . . . for other things. Poverty and ugliness. If only Edward . . . if only my husband could have lived to escape. . . . I can't tell you how awful it was to find money getting less, and less, and less. The house we took in Cornwall was horrible. I was ashamed to take Edward down to it, but at least it gave us room to have our own things round us. We went down there because he longed to be under his own doctor—the old family doctor, who'd retired in Cornwall— or rather, who'd gone to live down there because he had a delicate wife. I can never tell anybody how much he did for us. He was wonderful. Without him, I think it would have been . . ." She broke off, gave a rather uncertain smile and made a slight gesture as if raising her glass. "To forgetfulness," she said.

"To success," Gail corrected, and heard Mrs. Stratton laugh. It was a low, pretty sound.

"I'm a hundred years older than you are, but as we're going to see more of one another, would you consider calling me Anita? I shan't enjoy being Mrs. Strattoned all along the roads of the Basque country. Do you know that part of France?"

"Only slightly."

"I don't know it at all. I could never persuade my husband to go and stay at this cottage we're going to. He refused to consider spending winters out there. He wanted to be near Dr. Belldon, and as he relied on him so much—professionally and socially too—I couldn't bear to press him. I was dreading going out to it until I heard you were going to drive down to San Sebastian—I don't suppose you'd believe me if I told you that you've . . . rescued me. Without you, I would have found it almost impossible to hold out against Mrs. Westerby's insistence that I should go with her. Her godson's car, she told me, could quite well take three in comfort. I—I couldn't have borne it."

"Do you really have to go at the same time? Couldn't you have gone alone?"

"If I had, Mrs. Westerby would have found some good reason to follow me out. The cottage belongs to her and she pays the caretakers. I thought it better for us to go out together, especially as whatever furniture I don't want to keep, she wants to buy from me. I offered to give it to her, but she insists on buying it—that is, if I want to sell. She tried to persuade me to . . . don't think I'm being unkind, but there's no other word . . . to jockey me into driving out there with her. I said that I preferred to fly to Bordeaux, but I was quite certain she would insist on meeting me there and making me join them for the rest of the way. So when I heard you were going out there, or near there, it seemed like a lifeline—and I grabbed it. I'll try not to be a nuisance."

She stopped and put out her hand for Gail's empty glass.

"Shall I fix you another?"

"No, thank you. I've got to go back to the office after lunch."

"There's no time limit, I hope? I mean, you can stretch your lunch hour a little, can't you?"

"Mr. Frank was good enough to say so."

They laughed, and it occurred to Gail for the first time that Mrs. Stratton was not so very much older than herself; but her composure, and a certain staidness in her manner, widened the gap between them.

"Shall we go down to lunch?" Mrs. Stratton asked. "There's a main restaurant, but I thought it would be quieter to eat in the Regency Room. There shouldn't be many people there at this time."

Not many, but all millionaires, Gail noted, after a glance round the tables. Millionaires—and somewhat musty. The whole place, she thought suddenly, was out-of-date. And Mrs. Stratton was out-of-date. Success, instead of bringing her into line with the new, infinitely more informal way of life, had thrown her back; she was trying to buy—as everybody else in this overblown building was trying to buy—protection from the harsh winds of change. She was making up for the hard years by reaching backwards to a vanished world of leisure and luxury, imagining that she had found it in this setting. Gail eyed their fellow lunchers: two night-club owners, four film stars, half-a-dozen old women flashing diamonds. Money, money, money, she thought—not without a sense of outrage—her family, though illustrious, was impecunious.

The food was good, but the service, Gail thought, was geared to the semi-moribund clientele. The two smiling young waiters had obviously been trained to serve with smiling, unhurried grace. The inordinate delay between ordering and eating made Gail so irritated that she had to fight against a desire to thump her fist on the table and yell to them to bring on the funeral meats.

Mrs. Stratton, who seemed to suffer no pangs of hunger, opened her bag and put a card on the table beside Gail.

"Those are the times, in case I forget," she said. "The flight number and the time of arrival in Bordeaux. I thought it would be sensible to book a room at a comfortable hotel for the day—your car ferry arrives at dawn, and I shall be there before eleven. You must go to the Duchesse and have a good breakfast and I'll join you there. I've written down the address. You'll find a room booked for you."

This evidence of good organization was so different from Mrs. Westerby's haphazard plans that Gail found herself laughing.

"Share it," invited Mrs. Stratton.

"It isn't a joke—I was just thinking how difficult you must have found it to pin Mrs. Westerby down to times and places."

Mrs. Stratton raised her eyebrows.

"You've seen her since the reception?"

"I had to go and have lunch with her at her house. She had been talking to Mr. Frank about a paper her father wrote and I went to fetch it."

"Did you get it?"

"Not at first. Mrs. Westerby couldn't find it. That's why I laughed just now—at the contrast between the way you do things, and the way she does them. I rather like her," she added, for reasons not clear to herself.

"A great many people do. I think perhaps it's because she reminds people of one of those large, shaggy sheepdogs. I remember thinking, the first time I met her, that I'd have a lot of fun watching her. But"—a shadow crossed her face—"that wasn't quite the way it turned out." She raised her dark, rather mournful eyes to Gail's. "Did she talk about my . . . about her brother?"

"Yes, a little. She showed me a photograph."

"That is something I couldn't. . . . When someone has died, I think their photographs should be put away for a time. The ordeal of meeting them in a room, everywhere you turn, is. . . . Do you agree?"

"It depends," said Gail thoughtfully. "If you feel that way, it's silly to keep photographs lying around. My grandmother took the other view—that just because you're dead is no reason for sweeping away everything of yours that reminds people you're not there anymore. That sounds involved, but my brother and sister and I had our parents gazing at us from every corner of the room. Nice in one way, because we felt they were present—and they never changed, never grew old and ugly."

She forgot the subject of photographs in her relief at seeing food placed before her. Her appetite seemed out of keeping with the bored indifference shown by everyone else towards the delicacies on their plates.

Mrs. Stratton watched her with envy.

"I used to enjoy my food, once," she said. "I liked cooking, too—not dull, basic things, but exotic dishes. It wasn't much fun eating them alone. My husband only liked the plainest food, and later, of course, he could eat hardly anything. I learned to cook invalid dishes, and my meals were usually just finishing up what was left." She put down her fork and spoke slowly. "It was extraordinary, you know, to listen to Mrs. Westerby going on and on and on about this and that remedy for chest and lung complaints, when all the time . . ."

"Yes, I know. She told me."

"Perhaps I oughtn't to talk about her, or about him—but you've been drawn into this trip, and even though you're not doing more than taking me to the cottage, you're bound to learn a good deal about me, or about Mrs. Westerby, on the way. The trouble is that it's so difficult to mention her without seeming disloyal. The last impression I want to give you is that I didn't, or don't, like her. As I said, I was prepared to like her very much—but I don't think she ever reconciled herself to her brother's marriage. She came to visit us in Cornwall, but when my husband's health got worse, I felt—and sad to say, he felt, too—that she was better away from us."

"Is that why you went to live so far away?"

"Did she tell you that?"

"She gave the same reasons as you did," Gail said, "but was your real reason merely to get away from her?"

"I went," admitted Mrs. Stratton, "because Cornwall looked as far away as I could get from what I suppose we must call her kindly interference. She hasn't got much imagination, I'm afraid. She couldn't see that a sister looking after a bachelor brother was one thing. But a sister-in-law appearing with old family remedies and outdated advice and—worst of all—complaints about the treatment her brother was receiving—"

"She said you nursed him devotedly."

"She did?" Mrs. Stratton smiled. "That was nice of her. I nursed him devotedly because I loved him. But it would have been easier if she had been the kind of person who could have adapted herself to the new circumstances. I don't honestly think she was unduly possessive, although she—and his parents, too—treated him like a baby for so many years. I think she was just unable to see how very differently he felt about everything after his marriage. He was grateful to her, of course, but he was rather bitter about the fact that she and his mother had reared him in a semi-invalid atmosphere, protecting his lungs, which were perfectly sound, and neglecting his digestive organs, which were anything but."

Gail felt that part of the responsibility must be shared by the old family doctor, and remembered that Mrs. Westerby had mentioned him as one of the reasons for settling in Cornwall. She gave the question all the attention she could spare from cracking lobster claws—and then heard Mrs. Stratton answer it.

"In the end," she said, "nothing mattered—that is, no remedies would have done any good. It was wonderful to have Dr. Belldon—not only as a doctor, but as an old family friend, who could come in every day and talk about old days and old friends to Edward. He was wonderful."

"Was he at the reception? No." Gail answered the query herself. "No, he wasn't. I sent out the invitations, and there was no Dr. Belldon among them."

"I owe him all the comfort I'm enjoying now. It was he who first read my book. It was he who insisted on my letting him have it, so that he could show it to somebody who could judge it impartially. He brought it up to London when he came to visit some friends, and then he met Christopher Beetham and . . . well, you know the rest of it."

Gail wished that there could be less of Mr. Stratton and his last illness. The waiter was hovering, the vast menu was being offered once more—page three, chocolate mousse, peach ice and other things that Mrs. Stratton waved aside but that a working girl might put away without harm. It was bad luck about poor Mr. Stratton, but life had to go on.

Mrs. Stratton became aware of the waiter; she resumed her role of hostess and suggested fresh strawberries. Over coffee, she agreed reluctantly that Gail would soon have to go back to the office.

"When you're married," she said, "you'll look back and wonder why you looked forward to being free all day. I certainly did. Is this your first job?"

"Heavens, no! Fourth. Coffee bar—but I hated the hours. Model—but I hated the hanging about. Then secretary to a rather nice man who had something to do with wool—and now the Beetham Brothers."

"Boyfriends?"

"Nothing serious."

"There can't be any shortage."

"No. I'm lucky—or unlucky. Every friend of my brother's who passes through London is given a free pass to his share of the flat. They thump up the stairs—there's no lift—in the early hours, singing songs about Lulu-my-Lu. I've nearly been ejected twice."

"Evicted."

"Well—thrown out." She picked up her handbag. "I've really got to go. It's been a wonderful lunch—thank you so much."

"Don't lose the card I gave you."

"I'll remember anyway: the Duchesse at Bordeaux on the ninth of June. I ought to warn you that my brother's car is a bit rattly."

"I shall enjoy it—rattles and all. We might—"

She stopped abruptly, and Gail saw her eyes widen and then darken with anger. At the same moment, she heard sounds—sounds that were familiar. She did not need to look towards the door to know that Mrs. Westerby was making an entrance.

When she did look, she found the spectacle interesting—and instructive—it was clear that this was the one eventuality the Flamingo had not been prepared for: somebody whose appearance suggested she should be kept out, but whose accent and bearing proclaimed that she should be let in.

Mrs. Westerby did not wait for the management to make up its mind; she dealt with the headwaiter with the same easy authority she had shown towards Miss Teller.

"Out of my way, my good man!" she ordered in her most resounding boom. "No, I don't want lunch, thank you. I wish to speak to a relation of mine who— 'Oh, there she is! Anita, my dear, how lucky to catch you both."

She marched firmly towards her objective. She was dressed, to Gail's dismay, in the Robin Hood hat and the flowing dress. Her cloak was spotted with rain. She had draped two scarves and some beads about her neck, and she was wearing Oliver Cromwell's shoes. She looked even more grotesque than she had at the Beetham Brothers' reception.

"I wanted to catch Gail," she shouted. "Thank goodness you're still here, my dear. It's about the paper—you remember the little paper I promised to give your nice Mr. Frank? It's gone. I've hunted and hunted, and I can't find it anywhere. I can't imagine what—"

"You gave it to me," Gail said.

"I what?"

"You gave it to me when I went to lunch with you on Sunday."

"I gave you the little paper?"

"Yes."

"The one I said I would send to Mr. Frank?"

"Yes. I gave it to him on Monday morning."

"Then can you wonder," Mrs. Westerby asked everybody impartially, "that I spent this morning hunting in vain? Where did I find it, my dear?"

"In a drop-front desk."

"Extraordinary! And to think that I worried for nothing. I had made a promise, you see, and when I promise anything, I like to carry out my promise. What, I kept asking myself, would Mr. Frank think of me? And you say that all the time, he had it safely in his possession?"

"Yes."

"Then I broke in and interrupted your nice little lunch all for nothing. My memory must be going." Mrs. Westerby gave her head a hard thump by way of punishment. "I shall take myself off."

Mrs. Stratton had said nothing. She sat very pale and still, watching the furtive smiles on the faces of those seated at neighbouring tables. Now she looked up.

"Gail was just leaving," she said.

"Then perhaps she could drop me somewhere—we could share a cab."

"I'm going back to the office by bus," Gail said. "I can get from door to door, so it's not really worthwhile taking a taxi."

"Then I shall walk. It will do me good," Mrs. Westerby said. She retrieved the damp umbrella that a waiter had succeeded in wresting from her. "We shall meet at the cottage. Au revoir! Au revoir!"

Her exit was watched by every eye; amused smiles were on every face. Without a word, Mrs. Stratton rose and made her way to the door, Gail by her side. Mrs. Stratton had a rigid, almost a wooden, look.

"At her house"—Gail was struggling with a diminishing regard for Mrs. Westerby—"she seemed rather nice."

"Did she?" Mrs. Stratton asked mechanically.

"She was much quieter, and she wasn't wearing those awful. . . . I mean, she looked just like everybody else."

"That's rather hard to believe."

"I know she was pretty dreadful just now—and at the reception. There seems to be something about you that. . . . What I'm trying to say is that she seems to me to be doing her best to impress you, to—"

"She has succeeded in making a fool of me—twice. I suppose you told her you were lunching with me today?"

"Yes. I'm sorry."

They had reached the lift. Mrs. Stratton held out a hand and spoke in a warmer tone.

"Don't be sorry. I'm sorry I let her upset me and spoil the end of our nice lunch together. She's not trying to impress me, I'm afraid. I think she merely likes to be seen in my company. They say that success has its penalties. This is certainly a severe one."

Gail could not imagine Mrs. Westerby basking in anybody else's sunshine—but she did not say so. She went back to the office, and found Miss Teller waiting for her in her room.

"Well, how did the lunch go?" she asked.

"All right—until Mrs. Westerby burst in."

"To lunch—uninvited?"

"No. Just to tell me she'd spent the morning looking for the paper she'd already given me and which I'd already given Mr. Frank. Now tell me she's not crazy—in spurts."

"She's not crazy. What are you looking for?"

"The Stratton file."

"It isn't there. What do you want to know?"

"Nothing much—just the sequence of events."

"I can give you that. Book received by Christopher about the beginning of October. Husband died Christmas Day. Book read by us early January and accepted. After that the deluge—literally. But we had to go a bit slowly because of the recently-widowed angle. End of March, widow emerging, or recovering. Book business getting urgent. April . . . well, you've caught up now, I suppose?"

"Yes. Thanks."

"Now you can fill in for me. What's the idea behind this joint trip out to France? By joint I mean Stratton–Westerby. It's a long way to go, isn't it, just to look at furniture?"

"Not if it's all genuine Louis Quinze."

"And if it is, what's Mrs. Stratton going to do—ship it all home?"

"I don't know. Mrs. Westerby's going because she's in charge of the keys and the caretakers."

"And because she wants to be there to catch any crumbs that fall, I daresay. In other words, to retrieve any of the old family pieces that slip by Mrs. Stratton. Want some advice?"

"Not particularly, but go ahead."

"Don't let yourself get too involved with Mrs. Westerby."

"I'm not likely to. Why not?"

"I couldn't say, exactly. It's just a feeling I've had since that reception—something about her didn't seem to me to add up. Just you watch yourself."

Gail stared at her in amazement.

"You're not serious?"

"Yes, I am serious. I'm not trying to put lurid ideas into your head. All I'm saying is that if I were you, I'd watch Mrs. Westerby."

"In the intervals between watching myself?"

"You can laugh if you like, but you've known me long enough to credit me with some horse sense. What I'm telling you is simply this: That if you don't look out, you're going to get yourself too involved with this Stratton–Westerby setup."

And those, Gail admitted long afterwards, were the truest words anybody ever uttered.

Chapter Five

THE car ferry was full to capacity. The decks were thronged with noisy groups, some wearing armbands, others club badges to link them together. It seemed to Gail that she was the only person travelling alone.

In her cabin, a two-berth, she found no sign of a second occupant, and allowed herself a faint hope that she might be left alone; the berth was undoubtedly booked, but people missed boats, she mused hopefully, or changed their minds at the last moment, or died.

She was disappointed, but not surprised, to hear a voice outside shouting the number of the cabin—and then the door was thrust open and an enormous knapsack appeared, apparently without human support. Dangling from it were a tin mug, a large whistle, a water flask and an enamel basin. It dropped with a thump to the floor, revealing, framed in the narrow doorway, a squat, thickset woman in khaki shorts, khaki shirt and a khaki jacket. She looked incredibly muscular.

" 'Morning!" Having barked this abrupt greeting, she stood gazing round the small cabin. "Not much room, I must say. Going all the way?"

"No. Only to Bordeaux."

"Thank God for that. Can't stand people in with me. Shift that second case of yours, will you? Never understand why people have to travel with an entire trousseau. One of my women out there"—she jerked a chin towards the corridor and bent to unfasten the knapsack—"turned up with God knows how many bits and pieces. 'No, you don't, my good woman,' I said at once, 'no, you don't. The coach won't fit all that lot, so you'll have to leave half of it behind.' Left her calling me names. I'm used to that. You get used to anything, in this job."

She swivelled round in order to allow Gail to read the scarlet band, white-lettered, she wore round her left arm: *Organizer, Pontefield Hiker's Rally.* "This year, we're taking the coach to Leixoes. Then I drive it up to the port country and leave it in a garage, and we hike for ten days. Then home again. We've always got a definite objective— we don't just walk round the district looking at the scenery. We try to learn something. Last year, Tours and the Chateaux. Year before, Holland and the dykes. My own idea. I was the founder. Always a round dozen of us, all women. I won't be responsible for more than a dozen, and I won't take anybody without a fitness test. My name's Bluett. Married, but not living with him. Who are you?"

Gail told her.

"Staying at Bordeaux, or going on?"

"I'm going to San Sebastian."

"Driving?"

"Yes."

"Alone?"

"No. I'm meeting a friend at Bordeaux."

"Bad idea, if you ask me. You shouldn't tie yourself down if you're going on a trip—a private trip, that is. You can always pick up someone if you want company. Is this chap French?"

"No." Gail felt almost ungrateful at returning so little for so much, but decided to use the technique employed by her brother when faced by impertinent or unwarranted curiosity. "No, not French."

"Spanish, I suppose."

"Sort of mixture."

"You want to watch foreigners—but I daresay you're old enough to look after yourself."

Gail watched the contents of the knapsack being brought to light. She saw a small case containing papers, a plastic bag filled with toilet articles, one small and one large towel, one pair of very dirty white tennis shoes, two pairs of thick woollen socks, a crumpled map, a business-like looking ledger and some spare khaki clothing.

"I give them all a list and tell them that they've got to stick to it," Mrs. Bluett explained, throwing a few things into a drawer. "The vital thing is weight. What hope have you got of keeping to schedule if women overload themselves and drop behind? And yet here's this fool disobeying the rules before we even put a foot on the road. Staying long in San Sebastian?"

"It depends."

"Well, don't say I haven't warned you. I can't do more. Foreigners can let you down. Where did you come across this one?"

"As a matter of fact, he was a waiter at this hotel I was staying at in London."

"That's better than a hairdresser. Girl I know picked up a hairdresser and landed herself into a packet of trouble. Good-looking?"

"Oh, *very!*"

"They always are. Watch your money, that's all I can say. Has he got any?"

"Well, they always have at first, and they start off by *lashing* it out. But then somehow towards the end of the trip, they're—"

"Hauling it back again. The car's yours, I suppose?"

"No. As a matter of fact—"

"His?"

"No. It belongs to a Navy man. He let me borrow it, but I've got to take him back to England."

She saw dawning respect on Mrs. Bluett's face.

"Not getting in above your neck, are you?"

Gail said she hoped not, and watched the other woman march out in search of something to eat. Walking into the snack bar just after the ship sailed, she met a battery of a dozen pairs of eyes, and knew that her history had been recounted to the party of hikers.

She was glad to remember that there was always the certainty, when sailing from Southampton, of a brief interval during which travellers could brace themselves for the ordeal of the open sea. Gliding smoothly down Southampton Water, they could persuade themselves that the entire journey would be like this—decks level, rails drawing a straight line along the horizon. But the sea, for her, always seemed to have something grim in store—and this journey proved to be no different from any other. Only one night, but it was more than enough. Even the sight of the redoubtable Mrs.

Bluett—stretched, moaning and miserable on the opposite bunk, stripped of all her bombast—could not alleviate Gail's own suffering. Throughout the night, the waters tossed and the car ferry drove a relentless way through them at a steady twenty-two knots.

But morning came, and with it the strength to rise and dress and go limply out to look at Bordeaux. There was not much time to look; the car ferry stayed a mere hour and a half, pumping fuel in at pressure and sending cars off at speed.

From the dockside, Gail looked back at the ship and saw the Pontefield Hikers lining the rails, waiting to see her being met by a foreign mixture. Better to be thought abandoned in one sense than in the other, she thought, and glancing round, fixed upon a wild-haired, black-visaged young man lounging behind a pile of crates as the one most suitable to her purpose. Map in hand, she walked up to him, and for a few convincing moments could be seen leaning with him over the radiator of her car, map outspread, tracing a route. Dishonour satisfied, she drove away and turned south to find the Duchesse.

It was three miles outside the town, on a slope overlooking the estuary of the Garonne. Gail knew Mrs. Stratton well enough to be certain that it would be well-starred, but she was surprised, nevertheless, by the luxury of the room to which she was led. Mrs. Stratton was not due for three hours, and had been firm in her refusal to be met at the airport; the hotel, she had said, would send a car.

Two people arrived in a car just before lunch. Gail had bathed and changed and now, the horror of the night forgotten, was sitting on a shady terrace, making the most of a

long, cushioned chair, a cool, delicious drink and the exclusive attention of three whiteclad waiters. Not thus, she
mused, would she fare when she left Mrs. Stratton and
picked up Tim; inexpensive nightstops, roadside picnics and
fetch-it-yourself.

She saw the car stop under the glass porch of the hotel.
A man was at the wheel; beside him was a woman Gail
recognized as Mrs. Stratton. She rose and went to meet her
and saw her entering the hall escorted by two bellboys, a
hall porter and the tall, middle-aged and distinguished looking man with whom she had arrived.

When Gail approached, Mrs. Stratton turned with a
smiling welcome.

"Gail, how nice! Did you have a good journey?"

"Terrible. Waves like mountains."

Mrs. Stratton gave her soft laugh, and Gail thought for
the first time that she could be called beautiful; she looked
fresh and young and slim and composed, in a light wool
suit, her head bare.

The middle-aged man came to join them; Gail saw that
he was well-dressed, with a thin, tanned face. His manner
towards Mrs. Stratton was a mixture of deference and pro-
tectiveness.

"Gail, this is Sir Hugo Nevitt. Your nice Mr. Thomas
told him that I was travelling on the same plane, and asked
him to look after me. Sir Hugo, this is my young friend
Gail Sinclair." Sir Hugo bowed, smiled and conveyed, grace-
fully and convincingly, his pleasure at having Mrs. Stratton
as a travelling companion.

"But Mr. Beetham has made me very angry," he continued in his pleasant voice. "If he had thought of getting in

touch with me earlier, I could have driven Mrs. Stratton to the airport. My flat is barely four hundred yards from the Flamingo. You came over on the car ferry, Miss Sinclair?"

"Yes."

"I'm afraid I haven't your hardihood—I dodged the sea trip and came by air, and had a car waiting for me at the airport. I'm sorry it was so rough."

Gail had almost succeeded in placing him. The Nevett Commission—something to do with adult education. He was bringing out a book on his findings, or his theories, or both; that accounted for the tie-up with Mr. Thomas. There was something else. . . . Yes, Miss Teller had called him a sheep in wolf's clothing, but had not stopped to explain.

Mrs. Stratton was being conducted to her room; for clients who were only staying for one day, and not even a full day, Gail thought that they were being given a gratifying amount of service.

She went back to the terrace, and Sir Hugo followed her; he was lunching here, he explained, and Mrs. Stratton had very kindly agreed to let him join her. He said that he was on his way to Pau, to visit friends.

He sent away one of the chairs and selected another that he thought would be more comfortable for Mrs. Stratton, then ordered a drink for himself and for Gail.

"Mrs. Stratton is a charming companion," he said, leaning back and stretching his long legs on the footrest. "It is very sad . . ."

That, Gail told herself, was what she must keep remembering: how sad it was. She was on the sunny terrace of a hotel which the Michelin Guide awarded five little chateaux; she was sunk in foam rubber, drinking an expensive

chilled drink and awaiting a probably superb lunch—but it
was very sad. To remind her, there was that mauve suit.
Poor Mr. Stratton was dead and buried, and it was very sad.

The table at lunch overlooked a garden brilliant with
flowers. Lest Gail should feel herself left out—or because
Sir Hugo wanted to devote himself to Mrs. Stratton—a
young Frenchman who had got into conversation with them
on the terrace made a fourth at the meal. He was thin and
dark and amusing, and spoke almost perfect English. He
was on his way to Paris, but he gave Gail to understand that
he was ready to break his journey if there was any local fun
to be had.

"Why do you have to leave?" he demanded.

"I'm driving Mrs. Stratton," she explained.

He raised one eyebrow and glanced across the table, and
Gail agreed with everything he had not said: Sir Hugo's admiration was undisguised, and his car was at the door; by
all sensible standards a switch from Gail's car to his would
add to the pleasure of all parties.

It was difficult to gauge Mrs. Stratton's feelings. She
smiled at Sir Hugo and laughed gently at the Frenchman's
nonsense, but she retained the slight detachment Gail was
beginning to understand was characteristic. What was clear
was that the two—Mrs. Stratton and Sir Hugo—made a perfect pair. A perfect pair in a perfect setting, Gail decided,
and found herself wishing, to her surprise, that Mrs. Bluett
would walk in and drop her knapsack and provide an earthy
contrast to so much elegance.

She expected to drive away after lunch, but to her surprise, Mrs. Stratton went to sit on the terrace, and with her
went Sir Hugo. The Frenchman asked Gail what she pro-

posed to do, and was delighted to hear that she was going up to bed. It would take him all the way to Paris, she thought, to recover from the blow to his pride and to his nose when she banged the door on his expectant face.

She slept for an hour. When she went downstairs, she learned from Sir Hugo that he had been fortunate enough to get a room in the hotel at Chandon; they would be driving there in convoy.

The departure was impressive—only the chef, Gail thought, failed to appear. Her brother's car, standing behind Sir Hugo's, looked like a seedy interloper. Whether it was the fact that she had had no breakfast, followed by two drinks on an empty stomach, followed by a rich lunch, followed by a heavy sleep, Gail did not know; but as she got into the car beside Mrs. Stratton she found herself regretting having been caught up in this too-elaborate schedule. Plush hotels and baronets were all very well, but she could do without them on a Continental tour; she longed for her brother's easy, casual presence and their program of take-it-as-it-comes.

She drove fast. The road was good, the scenery not yet of the kind to draw the eye. The car was going well. An occasional glance in the mirror told her that Sir Hugo was keeping pace with her.

"How long are you going to stay in Chandon?" she asked Mrs. Stratton.

"I wish I knew. Not long, I think. I want to get home and onto house agents. The Flamingo was all very well to stay in for a time, but I must get into a house of my own."

"Where do you plan to live?"

"Oh, in London." Mrs. Stratton sounded surprised. "I

lived in London for years. I was living there when I met
Edward. We kept on my flat until we moved to Cornwall—
he wanted to keep it on longer, but it's as well we didn't—
it would have been an extra burden."

She fell into a reverie, and Gail only broke in on it when
she felt the air growing chilly.

"Not too cold?" she asked.

"Not a bit. I was just thinking that I can't remember
having driven in an open car before."

"If you feel it's too cold, we can always put up the hood."

She thought she had never before met anyone who fussed
so little. There was no fidgeting, no trite, irritating comments on the scenery, no forced conversation; there was in
fact no conversation at all. Mrs. Stratton settled into her
seat, folded her hands in her lap and gave herself up to en-
joyment.

She came out of a long silence to put a question to Gail.

"How did you like Sir Hugo?"

"He seemed very nice."

"He married one of the Degrelle sisters—have you ever
heard of the three beautiful Degrelle sisters?"

"Never."

"I hadn't, either. It's so difficult to know when to say
so, and when to pretend. I hate pretending, but when a
man tells you his ex-wife was a famous beauty, you hate to
say you never heard of her. I got out of it by murmuring
something or other. They're divorced. His house is lovely—
Mr. Thomas showed me some pictures in *Country Life*."
She paused and gave a sigh of pleasure. "Isn't it a heavenly
day? If only I could enjoy all this without the thought of
having to meet Mrs. Westerby at the end of it . . . but I
suppose you think I sound disloyal."

"Maybe I ought to murmur something or other."

Mrs. Stratton laughed. "Well, don't blame me too much. Over here, so far from England, I feel freer, more able to say things—even unkind things. I'm willing to grant Mrs. Westerby all the virtues: kindness, well-meaningness and all the rest. After that I can only say that I find her terribly embarrassing. How do you imagine I felt when she walked in, burst in, forced her way in to that reception or party or whatever it was, at the publishers? Did you welcome her when she waved a wet umbrella in the dining room of the Flamingo? I didn't."

"Do people really take much notice of eccentric characters?"

"It depends how close they are to the character. It's easy to smile at someone behaving oddly—as long as they're not with you, or related to you. I hate to be the center of a scene—I can't bear seeing everybody round me staring and grinning. I loathe any kind of public disturbance, any kind of scene. Don't you?"

"It depends. What our landlady calls a disturbance, my brother calls a mild party. It really does depend."

"Did you tell Mrs. Westerby we were meeting at the Duchesse?"

"I think I mentioned it to her godson."

"Then either he didn't tell her, or he kept her away," Mrs. Stratton decided. "That's a good sign. It shows that he can control her. What is he like?"

"Well . . . tall, quiet. Not much small talk, but not heavy-going. Grown-up."

"At thirty-four? You surprise me."

"Age is nothing to go by."

"That's true. Did he want to come on this trip?"

"No, I don't think he did."

"I sympathize with him."

She turned her gaze on the lovely scene, and it was some time before she spoke again.

"You're very quiet. What are you thinking about?"

"My mother," Gail said unexpectedly. "She and my father spent their honeymoon somewhere around here. I often wonder whether she knew what was ahead of her."

"What was ahead of her?"

"Travel. But she was a homemaker. We'd arrive somewhere—wherever my father was sent to—and she'd have the house fixed up in less than no time: curtains and flowers, and meals adapted to the country and the climate, and everything running like a dream. Then, as soon as we'd got to know the neighbours, my father would be transferred, and we'd pack up again. But my mother never stopped, never gave up, never thought it wasn't worthwhile. I suppose that's why I grew up believing that the most important thing of all is to make a home."

"Not every woman thinks so."

"Oh, I know. It's not an argument I can support, and I don't try. It just colours my outlook on men, that's all. I go for the home-lovers."

"I'm surprised one of the home-lovers hasn't persuaded you to make him a home."

"There's no hurry," Gail said, and was about to add that one was married for a long time, when she remembered that Mrs. Stratton had been married—twice—for a very short time.

"It doesn't do to have preconceived ideas on husbands,"

Mrs. Stratton went on, "but most women do. I had. At least, I had the first time."

"He was an actor, wasn't he?"

"Yes. But he wasn't a very good actor. His chief talent was running through money."

Gail said nothing; they drove on, every mile bringing them towards a peace and tranquillity that seemed to close round the car like a blessing. Towns and traffic seemed a thousand miles away. The only houses in view were Basque farmhouses with windows that blinked sleepily in the late sunshine. They passed oxen carts with picturesque yokes, lean figures in berets trudging beside them.

Some distance ahead, Gail saw that the road was being widened; soon a workman signalled her onto a oneway track. Above it, set pleasantly on a hillside, she saw a small café. A terrace in front of it was set with tables and a few cars were parked nearby.

"Would you like to stop for a drink?" she asked Mrs. Stratton.

Mrs. Stratton shook her head.

"Not unless you do."

"Then let's get on," Gail said, and ignored Sir Hugo's hopeful signals on his horn.

They passed a gang of workmen; the single track ended and Gail was flagged on by a grinning, grimy young workman who winked at her as the car went by. Round the next curve she saw a large, painted arrow pointing to a side road. She swung the car to the left and found herself almost immediately on a surface that made her slow to a walking pace. She looked dubiously at the rough track ahead.

"How much of this, I wonder?" she asked.

It was bad going. Mrs. Stratton braced herself as well as she could against the severe jolting. They passed piles of boulders on the hillside; above them, a party of roadworkers looked down at them and signalled; they were clearly indicating that the car was to go on and not go back, and Gail proceeded with more confidence. Feeling her way, she nosed along, avoiding the deeper ruts. Behind, mingling with the sounds coming from the workmen, she heard a shrill horn; glancing in the mirror she saw, far behind, Sir Hugo's car.

"That's all right, he's still behind us," Mrs. Stratton said. "We must be on the right track."

The horn sounded again—reassuringly, Gail thought. She kept on, but she began to wonder why a detour should send traffic so far off the main road. Ahead, she saw with some relief the roofs and chimneys of a small village; once there, she decided that she would ask for confirmation that she had not mistaken the route.

"The arrow *did* point to the left, didn't it?" she asked Mrs. Stratton.

"Oh yes." Mrs. Stratton spoke with complete certainty. "I think I know why we've been sent so far round. There was blasting going on—didn't you notice? This must be a safety measure."

It would hardly save their tires, Gail reflected, and wondered what she would do in the event of a puncture. The thought of Sir Hugo did nothing to reassure her; she could not picture the well-cut grey suit and the light straw hat bent over a greasy wheel.

She negotiated a narrow bend and drove into the little village. Her first impressions were of heat, loneliness and poverty; her next, that news of an approaching catastrophe had caused the inhabitants to flee, for not a soul was in sight. Then she saw figures appearing one by one at the doors of small, scattered houses and the shabby little café and the two or three wretched-looking shops. She was about to get out and ask for directions when Sir Hugo's car drew up behind her. In its wake came two more—the first, a large station wagon in which were two adults and two teenage children—and behind it, a very small red car containing two extremely stout passengers, a man and a woman.

Sir Hugo had got out of his car and was coming to speak to Mrs. Stratton. He looked annoyed.

"I'm afraid you—that is, Miss Sinclair—went off the route," he said. "I hooted, but you didn't stop." His eyes rested in displeasure on Gail. "Didn't you realize that this couldn't have been the right way to come? How could heavy traffic possibly negotiate that narrow track?"

"There was an arrow pointing this way," Gail said. "I thought it meant we were being detoured past the road works."

"Yes, yes, yes. So did I—at first. But I know these roads well, and after a few yards, I realized that there must be a mistake. I did my best to stop you, but you paid no attention to my horn. You went on."

The driver of the second car had got out and was approaching. He was a large, goodhumoured-looking man of about forty, with an easygoing, easyliving air. His accent was American.

"Off the track, I guess," he said laconically. "How come that arrow pointed this way?"

"I cannot tell you—but we must go back at once," Sir Hugo said. "There's obviously some mistake, but if we delay, other cars will follow us and there will be a serious bottleneck as they try to turn on the narrow road. We should go at once."

"I guess you're right," the American agreed, "but this guy"—he jerked his chin towards a man in workman's clothes who was approaching—"seems to have something to say about it."

The man began to speak before he reached them. Waving his hands in wide, angry gestures, he shouted something that Gail, in spite of her fairly sound knowledge of French, could not follow.

"Far as I can make out," the American said, "we should have read the notice."

"There was no notice," Sir Hugo said testily, and addressed the man in correct and dignified French. "There was no notice," he told him. "There was only an arrow which pointed this way."

"No." The man spoke emphatically, his lined, weather-beaten face red, his black eyes snapping. "No, the arrow pointed *that* way." He waved a hand toward the hills behind them. They should, he said, have gone *that* way, unless they wished to come to the village.

They had not, they told him, wished to come to this village. They would leave it at once.

Sir Hugo and the American both reached in their pockets for a tip; the man stretched out a calloused hand and pocketed both coins before releasing his last shattering piece of information. They could not go back. To go back now was quite impossible.

"I don't understand," Sir Hugo told him irritably.

"I do." The American, sounding more laconic than ever,

turned and called to his family. "Hey, Tag, you were right.
Tag," he explained, as the boy and girl scrambled out of the
car and came to join them, "Tag here, my son, always has
his eyes peeled, on the lookout for trouble. He told me I
ought to turn back, but—"

"But you didn't listen, did you?" The boy spoke in an
excited, triumphant tone. "You didn't listen, like you always never do. You kept right on—didn't he, Sharon?"

Sharon, as round and pretty as her brother was thin and
plain, said that yes, Pop had gone right on.

"That's right, I didn't listen," their father agreed amiably.
"And now I'm sorry."

As politely as his rising irritation would allow, Sir Hugo
asked to be informed what he was sorry about.

"Why, that I didn't listen to him. My name's Cotter, by
the way, Tagland Cotter. The lady in the car is my wife,
Nancy, and these are my kids, Sharon and Tag Junior." He
looked indulgently at his son. "Maybe someone can tell me
why this boy can always smell trouble a long, long way
away."

"It's remarkable." Sir Hugo spoke stiffly. "Quite remarkable. But I wonder if you would very kindly explain more
clearly what this trouble is that he—er—smelled?"

"The blasting, that's what," shrilled Tag. "Didn't you
see? That gang we passed—I told Pop they were all set to
blast. They shouted at us. They were trying to get us to
stop, I betcha."

"*Blasting?*" Sir Hugo looked stupefied. "But there was no
warning. There was no notice of any kind. Where was this
notice?" he turned to ask the workman.

But the workman was hard to find, for the inhabitants of

the village had by now grasped the reason for the presence
of so many foreign cars in their square. They were crowding
round to see, to hear, to comment and advise. As Sir Hugo
scanned the circle of faces, seeking his original informant,
he heard Mr. Cotter's voice.

"Oh-oh. More company. More tourists who can't read a
simple notice when it's stuck up in front of them."

"There was no notice," Sir Hugo reiterated angrily. "I
saw no notice of any kind."

"There wasn't one," said Mrs. Stratton quietly. "I was
sitting beside Gail looking out for signs. There was an arrow,
but there was no notice."

A sports car had driven up—a smart, blue and white two-
seater in which were a young man and a very small, extremely pretty girl with a sulky expression. The man intro-
duced himself breezily; he was Mark Stevens, English, and
this was Susie, his girlfriend, who was beautiful if you could
only see behind the scowl, and what the hell was the
holdup?

"We can't get outa here," Tag Junior told him. "We're
stuck. There was a notice to say don't come, 'cus they were
blasting, but we came right on, and now we can't get back,
see?"

It was not only a matter of seeing. Even as he spoke, there
was a prolonged booming sound. Breaking the dead silence
that fell upon the square came another, and then a third.

"Well, that's it," said Mark Stevens. "Blasting, just as
the boy said. But now that it's over, what's keeping us?"

"The fact"—Sir Hugo averted his eyes from Susie's generous display of leg and bosom—"simply the fact that the
road is now blocked. The notice, as far as I can make out

from this man's account, was posted to warn drivers that the road leading to this village would be blocked from now until they got the blockage cleared—which they seem to think will be early tomorrow morning."

"And in the meantime, we're stuck?" Gail asked.

"Quite so." Sir Hugo's tone told her that he held her personally responsible for the fact. "There is no passage for cars—only bicycles can get through. And I can only say that—"

He broke off, his attention for the moment given to a car that had appeared round the bend of the hill.

"Here comes another chap," Mark said, "who can't read a notice—if there was a notice. There won't be any more arriving after this. That last explosion must have just missed his taillight."

Gail was staring at the car—and as she recognized it, and the man driving it, she heard a sound beside her which told her that Mrs. Stratton had recognized the woman seated beside him.

"Oh . . . no! Oh Gail, no!" she breathed in a tone of horror. "It can't be. . . ."

Gail said nothing. Julian Meredith's car crawled towards them, bumping off one ridge to the next, lurching through potholes. And now Mrs. Westerby could be plainly seen. Her expression, when she saw Gail and Mrs. Stratton, was a mixture of astonishment, joy and commiseration. As soon as the car stopped, and before Julian could come round and open her door, she had alighted.

A sudden hush fell on the assembly. Mrs. Westerby was wearing an old-fashioned dustcoat that came almost to her toes. Her straw hat, small and basin-shaped and trimmed with raffia roses, was anchored by a gauze ribbon that ended in a jaunty bow beneath her chins. Beads rattled on the chains round her neck as Mrs. Westerby shouted.

"Anita! It isn't possible! Gail! How nice, how very nice—but how tiresome to be held up by this road-mending and sent round by this dreadful bypass. Now that we've met, we must drive on together. Ever since this morning, when I knew you would be setting off from Bordeaux, I hoped we would run into you. Not run into you—no, no, no—a pure figure of speech. It is wonderful to have come upon you like this."

Gail found herself swept without warning into a brief but warm embrace. Before Mrs. Stratton could take evasive action, her turn came and she was sucked into the vast, billowing bosom, emerging with a face so pale that Gail thought she was about to swoon—until she looked again and saw that the pallor was that of anger. Sir Hugo moved nearer; he and Mrs. Stratton acknowledged the introduction to Julian.

Julian's greeting to Gail was perfunctory; he was looking at the ring of spectators.

"Anything wrong?" he asked.

"Not an accident, I trust?" Mrs. Westerby said anxiously.

It was Mark Stevens who explained the situation to them. His manner showed plainly that he considered the holdup no hardship; he wasn't, he told them, going anywhere special; he and Susie were just going. The Americans also seemed unperturbed; Tag Junior and his sister were taking turns at riding the village donkey, while their mother took photographs. The two occupants of the small red car had produced a flask and some sandwiches and were having a standup snack.

Sir Hugo looked round with ill-concealed anger. He did not want food or photographs; he wanted to get back to the main road, failing which he wanted the blood of the workman who had neglected to display the notice where drivers could see it.

"I shall bring this to the notice of the authorities," he said.

"That's fine." Mr. Cotter spoke soothingly. "You do that. But right now, I guess we ought to start looking for some place to sleep tonight."

"Stranded!" Mrs. Westerby appeared to have at last grasped the full import of the situation. "Marooned!"

Julian looked at Gail.

"You were misled by the arrow, too?" he asked.

"We were all misled," Sir Hugo told him angrily. "Why else are we here? The only reason there isn't a trail of cars following yours is that the block must have occurred shortly after you drove off the main road."

"Now I understand!" Mrs. Westerby exclaimed. "I noticed that the car behind ours was stopped by a party of workmen. When I looked again, I saw the car turning back. I would have mentioned it to Julian if I hadn't been so certain that we were following the direction indicated by the arrow. I'm not going to pretend that I'm too distressed about it, because it's such a pleasure to have met my sister-in-law. Anita, as we are all fellow-strandees, I think we had better make ourselves known to everybody. I am Mrs. Westerby, from Sussex, England. This is my godson, Julian Meredith. Mrs. Stratton is my sister-in-law. She is travelling with Miss Gail Sinclair."

She paused expectantly, and the others made themselves known. To each, Mrs. Westerby offered a word, in the man-

ner of one giving out prizes. She remembered that Sir Hugo
had married one of the pretty Degrelle sisters—Laura, wasn't
it? She had known them as children and had always thought
Laura the prettiest. Laura was not travelling with Sir Hugo?

Sir Hugo said that he was travelling alone; the way he
said it made Mrs. Westerby lower her voice and lean forward to address him in an anguished tone.

"Not . . . dead?" she breathed. "Have I been tactless?
Have I wounded you?"

Sir Hugo, looking at her with hatred, said that his wife
was not dead. Mrs. Westerby, sighing with relief, turned
to Mr. Cotter, patted the unappreciative Tag Junior on the
head, told Sharon sympathetically that fifteen was always an
awkward age, and informed her mother that she would have
taken her for an Englishwoman.

"My wife," Mr. Cotter said hastily, seeing his wife's expression, "isn't English. She comes from an old Southern
family. A very old Southern family."

Mrs. Westerby bowed, and turned to study the stout couple chewing beside their car.

"German?" she ventured. "I thought so. Mr. and Mrs.
Guzzman? How do you do? And you"—she turned to Mark
and Susie—"are sister and brother?"

"God forbid," said Mark. "Look, how would one get a
drink in this place?"

"Before we drink, let's fix some place to sleep," Mr. Cotter suggested.

Mrs. Stratton, standing pale and silent beside Sir Hugo,
glanced at him as though waiting for him to take charge of
affairs. But it was Mrs. Westerby who assumed command.
Turning to the bystanders, she spoke in a patois that was
understood by none of her fellow travellers.

"I am speaking to these people," she explained, "in the way the Basques in this part of France speak—the way I learned to speak to them as a child. I have been asking about accommodation for the night. There is an inn—that building over there. This is the landlord"—she indicated a small, shrunken figure—"who says that he can offer five rooms only, three of them facing the hillside and the other two facing this way—rather small, but with a balcony."

"Count me out," Mark said at once. "Susie and I carry a tent."

Mr. Guzzman, in halting English, enquired what was to be done about those who would not be able to stay at the inn.

"I think we ought to draw lots," Mr. Cotter said. "We can put numbers into a hat—if anybody's got a spare hat— and we draw a room at the inn, or we don't. From the look of it, the place won't be much more comfortable than any of those other houses over there."

"I think they're pretty." Sharon looked round at the scattered little Basque-type dwellings. "I'd like to stay in that one with the cows."

"She means she'll stay inside and the cows'll be outside— I think," her father explained. "Well, now let's get this lottery started."

Mrs. Westerby had already produced another small round hat, and was extracting visiting cards from a small silver case. She began to count the company.

"The Guzzmans, Anita, Sir Hugo, Mr. Stevens—no, not Mr. Stevens—Gail, Julian, myself, the Cotter family. Mr. Cotter, how many rooms do you require?"

"We usually take one large and two small, but I guess this time, we'll take what we can get," he told her.

"There is no shortage of accommodation in the village," said Mrs. Westerby, "but everybody must take his meals at the inn. Mr. Cotter, we shall count your family as one unit, I think."

"Just as you say," he agreed equably.

"I shall leave five cards blank. Those who draw the five blanks will be entitled to choose a room at the inn. The others, I'm afraid, will have to go elsewhere. Does everybody agree to this?" Mrs. Westerby asked.

Nobody disagreed. Using the radiator of Julian's car as a table, she took her pen and wrote briefly on the back of some of the cards.

"I am simply putting crosses," she looked up to explain. "Five blanks, and the rest crosses."

She folded the cards in two and in two again, and dropped them into the hat.

"Will you please," she requested, walking up to the waiting line, "open your card as soon as you draw it. I shall begin at this end and work along the line until all the blanks are drawn. Anita?"

Mrs. Stratton took a card and unfolded it. The landlord of the inn drew near, ready to welcome his guests. The local inhabitants formed a semi-circle at a respectful distance, looking like underprivileged lions waiting to be thrown a few scraps of gladiator.

"A blank," said Mrs. Stratton, and held up her card.

"Lucky for you," said Mrs. Westerby, peering at it. "Sir Hugo?"

"Please draw your own first," he said stiffly.

"Oh, thank you."

She drew a card, opened it and gave an exclamation of annoyance.

"Mine is blank," she said, and held it up for all to see. "I'm not going to pretend I shan't be more comfortable at the inn, instead of having to walk up and down the hill to get to dinner and breakfast, but I do feel rather like the woman who won her own raffle. Sir Hugo?"

He drew a blank card, and Mrs. Westerby spoke irritably.

"I haven't shaken them up enough. Please wait." She shook the hat vigorously. "That's better. Now we can go on."

The Guzzmans and Gail came next; they also drew blanks, and Mrs. Westerby turned to the rest of the party.

"The inn is now full, but I think you will all get quite good rooms at the other houses," she said. "Let me tell you where they are. This man"—she detached him from the crowd—"offers a room in his house, which is the one over there. This woman is the owner of the shop at the end of the square. She offers two rooms. In that pink house on the hill there's a room—this woman will show it to anybody who would like to inspect it."

She walked toward the inn, and after a slight hesitation, Mrs. Stratton and Sir Hugo followed. Mr. Guzzman stared after them with a frown of bewilderment, and then turned to address Julian.

"This lady, this big lady, you are akin to her?" he asked. "A grandson, maybe?"

"Godson."

"This blanks, I don't understand."

"Drawing a blank, the way I always figured it," Mr. Cotter said, "meant . . . well, drawing a blank. This time it was different. This time, if you drew a blank, you were in. See?"

"No."

"It is very simple," Mrs. Guzzman told him. "The gentleman just *told* you. You did not keep your head on what he was saying. The blanks . . . he explained all that."

"If you and your wife would like my blank," Gail said to Mr. Cotter, "I'll be happy to—"

"No, thanks. It's real kind of you, but I guess four of us would have taken up practically all the hotel rooms," he said. "We'll go along with this fellow here."

He led his wife away; the children were already halfway up the slope, riding the donkey. Julian handed Mrs. Westerby's luggage to the landlord of the inn and drove to a distant house, its owner crouching nervously in the seat beside him.

Gail went into the inn. At a telephone at the end of the corridor she could hear Sir Hugo giving somebody a piece of his mind—a French piece. The matter, he was informing his listener, would be taken up at a high level by him personally; he would see to it that the highway authorities were called to account.

The landlord appeared and led Gail upstairs to one of the rooms opening on to a narrow balcony. There was no partition separating her half of it from that of Mrs. Westerby, who was in the room next to hers. Across the small, dark, uncarpeted landing was Mrs. Stratton's room and, next to it, the Guzzmans'; next to them was Sir Hugo.

There was only one bathroom; Mr. Guzzman got to it first and stayed in it so long that his wife went to pound protestingly on the door. Gail changed into slacks and a sweater, took a wooden chair onto the balcony and sat

down, pad on knee, to scribble a letter to her sister. Below
her she could see the roughly-terraced entrance on which
the landlord was busy placing a few small, round tin tables
and chairs.

She looked up as Mrs. Westerby came out onto the balcony.

"Comfortable?" she asked.

"My dear, I never allow discomforts to worry me. I daresay I shan't sleep a wink on that bed—it's years since I came
across one of those feather mattresses—but I do so hate people who grumble, unless grumbling can alter things. Sir
Hugo"—she leaned forward and lowered her voice—"is *furi-
ous*."

"I know. He was on the phone when I came in, telling
them who he is."

"He began to tell me that you had led him into this by
refusing to stop when he sounded his horn. I told him not
to talk nonsense. Anita, I'm glad to say, seems to be taking
it all extremely well. She— Oh, here's Julian coming." She
leaned perilously over the low railing. "Julian, come on up
and look at my room. What is yours like?"

He had changed into a shirt and jeans; his hair was damp.
He glanced up and spoke briefly.

"Needs new straw," he said.

He came through Mrs. Westerby's room onto the balcony.

"Straw apart," Gail said, "what's it like?"

"It's got a nice, clean animal smell. If there has to be a
smell, that's the smell I like to have. The river runs past the
end of the garden—I had a quick bathe in it. Cold, but nice
and fresh."

"Has anybody any idea when we shall be able to get away tomorrow?" Gail asked him.

"Stevens and Susie seem to be in the know. Their tent's behind the house of the brother of the man whose sister's married to the foreman in charge of the blasting operations. They get their news straight from the tunnel's mouth, and they say the road'll be clear about nine tomorrow. Tag Junior's got his own sources of information and he agrees with that."

"He's a very intelligent little boy," Mrs. Westerby said.

"He is," agreed Julian. His face was expressionless. "He reckons the draw was rigged."

"The draw was . . . Oh, I see what you mean. Yes, of course he would think that," Mrs. Westerby said. "Everybody but the prizewinners always think that. Why, everybody saw me arranging it! There was no concealment of any kind whatsoever, and if that little boy says there was, he should say it to me."

"He didn't say there was any concealment whatsoever. He just said the draw was rigged. Where did Sir Hugo join you?" he asked Gail.

"The publishers asked him to keep an eye on Mrs. Stratton on the plane. So he did. Then he decided to go on to Chandon. He's got a room at the hotel there."

"Actually got it, or hopes to get it?" Mrs. Westerby enquired. "It's usually full for the whole of June."

"He got in," Gail said.

"Then he was very lucky." Mrs. Westerby rose from the wicker chair on which she had been seated. "I'm going inside. I think the bathroom is free at last. I can have a bath, and then—" She stopped, her eyes on two figures who had appeared on the terrace below them. Sir Hugo and Mrs. Stratton left the inn and walked slowly along the path that wound round the foot of the hill. "No, I've changed my mind . . . I shall have my bath later," she ended. "A little walk will do me good."

Gail and Julian watched her marching determinedly after the retreating pair; she caught up with them and there was a short halt, and then the three figures went on in Indian file along the narrow track.

"Maybe she thinks it's too soon after Edward," Gail murmured. "Do you like her—Mrs. Stratton?"

"She isn't at all as I'd pictured her."

He said no more. They saw the Cotters appearing from a distant house, carrying towels and walking down to the river. Mark Stevens and Susie emerged from their blue nylon tent and hurried to join them. From across the landing could be heard a low, regular snoring: Mr. and Mrs. Guzzman at rest.

"I suppose we go on in convoy tomorrow," Julian said into the silence.

Gail hesitated.

"No, not in convoy," she said at last. "I think Mrs. Stratton would rather we went separately."

"Wasn't Sir Hugo trailing you on the way here?"

"Yes. I'm going to try and shake him off tomorrow."

"He won't like that."

Gail stared at him.

"You and Mrs. Westerby—both of you—don't like him hanging round her, do you? I suppose you think it's too soon, too. Or do you just feel you ought to be on Mrs. Westerby's side."

"Who's talking about sides?"

"I am."

"Then don't. Wait till there's a row before you start talking about taking sides."

She felt her temper rising, but before she could speak, her attention was caught by the sound of a motorcycle. Watching it as it approached the inn, she saw that two men were seated on it—one was a workman still dressed in dusty clothes. The pillion passenger was a policeman.

"What's a *gendarme* doing here?" she asked. "He looks angry."

The motorcycle stopped. The *gendarme* got off; in his hand was a length of material which he shook out and waved wrathfully at the workman.

"This—you see?" he said. "Now we shall find out."

Gail's eyes fixed themselves on the dangling remnant; slowly she recognized it. She opened her mouth to speak, and felt Julian's hand gripping her arm warningly. Glancing at him, she saw to her amazement that he was staring down at the two men with something like fear on his face.

They were not more than fifteen feet above the rough terrace on which the men were standing. Julian took a cautious step backwards, drawing her with him and motioning her to silence. They heard the *gendarme's* summons to the landlord; they heard him explaining the reason for his visit, and they knew that he was waving the piece of material as he spoke. This, he said, had been found wrapped round the notice which had been placed beside the road to warn motorists of blasting, and telling them not to approach the village unless they intended to stay in it. This, and not a workman's mistake, was the cause of the trouble. This was a scarf, and this Englishman who had complained would be able to judge whether it belonged to a poor workman. This was a woman's scarf; a foreign woman's scarf. Find out who owned this, and you would find a madwoman—for who but a madwoman would wind a scarf round a warning notice?

Gail's eyes met Julian's; he seemed to be asking her how much she understood. The answer was on her face.

The landlord, impressed but nervous, said that the Englishman was out walking; he would return soon, and the matter would be dealt with. There was no need for the workman to wait; he could go home. He, the landlord, would get out his motorcycle later to take the policeman back—but first there was time for him to have a drink.

The workman went away; the *gendarme* sat down at one of the tables. On the balcony, Gail and Julian stood silent and motionless. She did not know what he was thinking; her own mind could grasp only one shattering fact: The scarf was Mrs. Westerby's.

She stood trying to clear the confusion from her brain. She heard the scraping of a chair, and with Julian, peered over the railing. They saw the table, and on it a crumpled scarf, half-hidden by the policeman's hat. The policeman had gone into the inn.

What followed was so swift that she was never fully able to believe that it had taken place. The silence, the speed, above all the success of the action combined to make her feel that she had acted in a dream. She saw Julian go into the bedroom and look round desperately and then seize and detach the cord that held back the woven curtains. At one end was a metal hook. He leaned over the railing—lower and lower—and then it became clear that the cord would not reach the table below. Without warning, he drew Gail forward and pushed the cord into her hand. The next moment he had caught her by the waist, upended her and hung her over the balcony, holding her thighs in a hard grip.

Helpless, outraged, she nevertheless endeavoured to retrieve the scarf. The hook dangled, slipped and then gripped; she pulled, and the scarf moved. But for all her efforts to move it gently, it dislodged the *gendarme's* hat and sent it rolling to the ground. After that there was nothing to do but draw up hook and scarf and wait for Julian to release her.

On her feet once more, she faced him with eyes blazing with anger—but he gave her no time to speak. He drew her into the bedroom, restored the curtain cord to its place and thrust the scarf into the pocket of his jeans. As he did so, a commotion broke out below.

They listened. How, the *gendarme* wanted to know, could so light a wind have whisked the scarf out of sight? But how else could it have gone? Could it fly by itself? the landlord demanded. The evidence had gone, blown away; without it, the story sounded too thin, too fantastic to be worth recounting to the Englishman. It would be better to go away and say nothing.

The *gendarme* wrestled with the problem; Gail faced her own. She was quite certain that the scarf was Mrs. Westerby's; she was equally certain that it was the scarf that had been wrapped round the warning notice. If Mrs. Westerby had put it there, she could also have turned the arrow to point in the wrong direction. And appalling as these thoughts were, it was obvious that Julian shared them.

Below, the arguments continued, but with diminishing force, and at last it was agreed that, without the evidence, there was no point in waiting to confront the angry Englishman. The best thing would be to go away and forget the incident.

The landlord fetched his motorcycle; the *gendarme* clambered on to the pillion seat; the sound of the engine faded into the distance.

"And now," Gail said, "we can talk."

"There's nothing to talk about," he said. "I'll be glad if you'll say nothing to anyone about what happened just now."

She stared at him, stupefied.

"Say nothing about . . . say nothing . . . ?"

"That's right. Say nothing to anybody."

"You know as well as I do," she said, "that that scarf belongs to your godmother. It's Mrs. Westerby's, and she—"

"I recognized it, and didn't want to involve her in any kind of questioning—and so I tried to get hold of it, and with your kind help, succeeded. And as far as you're concerned, that's all there is to it."

"You mean I've got to accept, calmly and without saying anything to anybody, the fact that your godmother's scarf was found wrapped round a notice telling us all to keep away from here? I'm entitled—we're all entitled to know just *how* it got wrapped, aren't we? We're all entitled to ask questions."

"I'll ask all the questions."

Her eyes narrowed.

"You realize what you're saying, don't you?" she asked. "You're admitting that Mrs. Westerby did it."

"I'm admitting nothing whatsoever. I'm merely asking you not to start a trail of rumor that might lead to trouble."

"But you believe she did it."

"I think it's fantastic to suggest anything of the kind."

"So do I. But fantastic or not, it's her scarf, and I saw your face when you realized—"

"Could I persuade you to mind your own business?"

"This is my business. I'm stuck in a beastly inn in a seedy French village and as far as I can see, it's your godmother who got me here. If she wrapped a scarf round a warning notice, she's crazy—and it isn't the first time I've thought so."

"As she isn't crazy, we can assume that she didn't have anything to do with it."

"If she isn't, then she knew what she was doing. And if she knew what she was doing—"

He walked to the door and opened it.

"Would you mind continuing this cross-examination outside?" he asked.

She hesitated—and then she went downstairs and he followed her. Outside, all was quiet. They walked slowly towards the river, and saw the two American children floating on an improvised raft; the grown-ups were collecting towels and preparing to leave. From the nearby woods came Mrs. Stratton and Sir Hugo; Mrs. Westerby was between them.

Gail sank on to a patch of grass warmed by the last rays of sunshine, and stared at the slowly approaching trio.

"I don't understand," she said. "I don't understand anything."

"Do you have to understand?" Julian asked.

"I can't be left hanging in midair, can I? I've got to think

—I've got to work things out—and if you refuse to help me, I have to work them out my own way. I think that scarf was wrapped round the notice. It's your godmother's scarf. If she didn't do it, the scarf must have been stolen from her."

"Not necessarily. It could have blown out of the car. If you weren't disposed to jump to conclusions, you'd see that there could be several explanations."

She made no reply. Julian's eyes were on the approaching figures, but she could read nothing from his expression.

"Julian, how lazy of you!" Mrs. Westerby called as they came near. "We've been for a splendid walk while you two have just sat about. Go and stretch your legs—you've been cramped up in cars too long."

"Any news about the road-clearing?" Julian asked.

Sir Hugo answered; he looked sullen, and less assured than he had done earlier in the evening.

"We should be able to leave early tomorrow morning," he said.

A deep breath, not quite a sigh, came from Mrs. Stratton.

"Tired?" Gail asked.

"Very," Mrs. Stratton said, and there was a kind of desperation in her voice. On an impulse prompted by pity for her, Gail heard herself speaking words she had not meant to utter.

"Has anybody lost a scarf?" she asked.

"Did you find a scarf?" Mrs. Stratton asked in her turn.

"Yes." Gail looked at Julian, and he drew it slowly from his pocket. "A man brought it. He found it on the road. He—"

"Mine!" Mrs. Westerby shouted. "Mine!" She took the scarf from Julian's hand and tried to shake out the creases.

"Ruined, I'm afraid. Julian, I hope you gave the man some small reward?"

"Where did you lose it?" Julian asked.

"I always think that's such a *silly* question," Mrs. Westerby said. "To know where one lost a thing is nearly always to know where it is—unless it has been removed or stolen. I can only tell you that the last time I had this scarf was when you and I, Julian, were sitting on the terrace of that little café—do you remember? The one we stopped at just a little way before the road-mending. I left you for a moment, and I had it with me. I daresay the wind whipped it off and carried it away—it's very light, as you see. How much did you give the man who found it?"

"I didn't give him anything."

"You should have done, my dear boy. It was very honest of him to have brought it back. It's only a scarf, but scarves can be worth quite a lot of money."

Gail opened her mouth to tell her where the scarf had been found—and then something on Julian's face made her close it again. Examining her feelings, she found that she was less anxious than she had been earlier to discover the truth. She had an uneasy feeling that she was on the fringe of something dark and tangled; the less she knew, she decided suddenly, the less possibility there was of her being drawn in. She regretted her impulsive mention of the scarf.

Mrs. Stratton and Sir Hugo were going towards the inn.

"We shall all meet at dinner," Mrs. Westerby called to them. "I've told the landlord to arrange a table in a nice corner for the five of us. A warm corner," she added to Gail and Julian. "Once the sun goes down, you'll find it remarkably chilly. Did you think Anita looked a little tired? I did.

I hope she'll get a good rest tonight. And now, my dears, shall we sit down and have a drink before getting ready for dinner?"

Julian did not move.

"The scarf," he said slowly, "was found wrapped round the notice warning people not to come to this village."

Mrs. Westerby stared at him in the utmost astonishment.

"Round a notice, did you say?"

"Yes."

"My scarf—this scarf—was wrapped round it?"

"Yes."

"Then that explains everything," Mrs. Westerby said. "*That's* where it went. It was obviously whipped from round my neck—being of such soft material, I wouldn't feel it go —and it was carried by the wind until it reached an obstacle, and then became entangled round it. Have you ever *heard* anything so extraordinary?"

"Never," Gail said.

"And when you *think*"—Mrs. Westerby spoke in an awed tone—"when you think what might have happened if the notice had warned of some real danger! Thank Heaven it was only a temporarily blocked road, and nothing worse. How horrible it would have been. . . ."

She shuddered—a tremor that shook her enormous frame. Gail, staring at her, felt a kind of fascination creeping over her. Her thoughts, usually so clear, so easy to marshal, blurred before the combination of the known and the feared; Mrs. Westerby's face, by now so familiar, was a face on which she could read no more than its owner cared to write. She could tell herself that Mrs. Westerby was nothing but what she appeared to be—ugly, kindly, awkward and blundering—harmless. But she could not make herself believe it—not when Julian's white, set face made her certain that he was struggling against suspicions far more serious than her own.

They watched Mrs. Westerby going into the inn.

"Satisfied?" Julian asked, as she disappeared into the dark entrance.

"I'm sorry I mentioned the scarf. I spoke before I could stop myself."

"It's a dangerous habit. Are you still convinced she's crazy?"

"No."

"What made you change your mind?"

"If she'd suddenly gone crazy and wrapped her scarf round the notice, she wouldn't have been able to talk about it so reasonably. And if for some mysterious reason of her own she *did* do it, she would have asked us—wouldn't she? —to say nothing to the others."

"Are you going to say anything about it to the others?"

"Not if you don't want me to."

"I don't want you to. All I want you to do is forget the whole thing."

"I won't do that. If you want to know what I think—"

She hesitated.

"Well?" he asked.

"If I were you, I'd . . . I'd keep an eye on her." She stopped and turned slowly to face him. "Is that why you came out with her? Is that why you agreed to drive her out to the cottage? To . . . to keep an eye on her? To watch her, to see that she didn't . . . that she. . . . Well, just to keep an eye on her?"

There was a long silence.

"Yes," he said at last. "That's why."

Chapter Six

NOTHING could have looked more peaceful than the countryside as dusk fell and the Cotters, with Mark and Susie and the children, came strolling over the quiet hillside towards the inn for dinner. Mr. and Mrs. Cotter went into the house in search of drinks. Mark Stevens followed them, leaving Susie with Gail at one of the small, round tin tables. Sharon and Tag Junior sat at the one next to them.

"Awful hole to be stuck in," Susie commented sulkily. "I told Mark not to come down that road. I told him twice, but he wouldn't listen." She frowned at the children, who were executing a rhythmic drumming on the table top. "Hey, you two—shut up!" She resumed her complaints to Gail. "This village gives me the creeps. You wouldn't think there was a main road not far from it, leading out to civilization. I don't suppose any of these characters ever got as far as the main road. When do we eat?"

"Soon," Gail assured her.

"I'll be glad when we get out of here."

"Well, I won't," said Tag. "I'd like to stay here. I wish we could go on being stuck. I'm sick of moving around. We do it all the time. I wanna go home, but we never will." He sounded bitter. "I bet we never will."

"Holidays come to an end," Gail offered as comfort.

"Holidays? Who said holidays?" he demanded. "This is work—my dad's work. Don't ask me anything about what he does. All I know is he has to do it in a lotta places. We're supposed to have a place to stay in Paris, but do we ever get to stay in it? No, we don't. We just move around all the time. I'm glad we're stuck, for once. But tomorrow morning, goodbye, nice to have met you."

"Oh, you're always grinding away at something," his sister said in disgust.

"I know how he feels," Gail said.

"Oh no, you don't," Tag answered. "*Nobody* knows how I feel. Everybody's always giving off that junk about travel's-good-for-you. Travel's ed-u-ca-ting. Why didn't they leave me in school back in the States, and let me get educated there? I wanna *stay* some place . . . just *stay*, that's all."

"I used to feel that way," Gail told him.

"You did?" He came to her table and gave her his full attention. "Did you get dragged around when you were little?"

"My brother and sister and I—yes."

"All round France, like me?"

"Worse. Brazil, Mexico, Peru, Chile. Until I was about ten."

"And then what?"

"My parents died and we were sent to live with my grandmother. After that it was just home and school."

Tag Junior sat gazing into this bright future. He was about to say something when Mark came out carrying a tray of drinks.

"I had to guess what Julian wanted," he told Gail. "Where's he got to?"

Tag Junior pointed towards the hillside.

"Here he comes."

Julian, joining them, took the drink gratefully.

"Sorry to leave you to do it all," he said. "You all looked so clean that I got out of my jeans into trousers. And I had a phone call to make."

"Lovely London?" Susie asked wistfully.

"No. Paris. The only place I ever saw a phone like this one was in an old western."

Mrs. Cotter strolled outside.

"Kind of a flood upstairs," she remarked.

"What kind of flood?" asked Tag Junior.

"Bathwater," his mother said. "It's on its way to your room," she told Gail. "I guess you'd better go on up."

Tag Junior had already gone to investigate. He returned at high speed and addressed Julian.

"Hey," he said. "It's that old lady—your aunt or something. She's burst one of the pipes, it looks like."

Julian put down his glass and followed Gail, who was already hurrying up the stairs. As they went, they had to keep close to the wall in order to avoid the channels of water coursing down into the hall.

They reached the landing to find the landlord on his knees helping the maid to mop the floor. Both were protesting loudly. The bathroom door was wide open; in the doorway, wearing a long, green cotton dressing gown and a mobcap made of towelling, stood Mrs. Westerby. She was protesting as loudly as the landlord and brandishing a piece of metal which Julian, picking his way through the rivers of water, took from her and identified as part of a brass tap.

"Now look, Julian," she continued without pause her stream of explanations. "Now you can see! Am I to blame if the tap comes away in my hand? Because that is precisely what happened. I could hardly get the thing to turn on. Having turned it on, I found the water coming out with far too great a force, and so I attempted to turn the tap the other way. I couldn't. You can see for yourself how small the bathtub is. The water filled it in no time, but before I could come out and call for assistance, I had naturally to put on my robe. By that time, everything had overflowed." She waved a hand. "As you see."

The water had rushed below the ill-fitting door of the bathroom and spread out into three divergent streams. One had made its way under the door of Sir Hugo's room; Sir Hugo, in shirtsleeves in his doorway, was holding up a pair of shoes and a pair of slippers which had been soaked before he noticed the flood, and addressing Mrs. Westerby in a voice choked with anger. Mr. Guzzman, uttering loud cries of distress, was flinging garments out of a canvas hold-all that had become saturated with water. The Cotters were downstairs in the hall, clearing everything from the path of the descending streams.

Julian snatched a mop and diverted a tributary that was snaking its way into Gail's bedroom. Going to his assistance, Gail glanced across the landing. Mrs. Stratton was standing outside her room, saying nothing, her eyes going slowly round the scene. They came to rest at last on the still-protesting Mrs. Westerby. There was a look in them that Gail would have given much to be able to identify. Mrs. Westerby met the look and fell abruptly silent. For a few moments the two women stared at one another; then Mrs. Stratton turned and went into her room and closed the door.

"She blames me," Mrs. Westerby said angrily. "You can see she blames me. Everybody blames me. Why can't you explain, Julian, that accidents of this kind can happen to anybody? It might have been Sir Hugo who was having a bath just as the tap chose to give trouble. He would have been just as helpless as I was to stop the flow. He would have had to wait, as I had to, for the landlord to fetch a tool of some kind. I am sorry, my dear Sir Hugo, about your wet shoes, but I cannot really understand why you should direct all your annoyance at me. You might remind yourself that—"

There was no point in going on; Sir Hugo had gone into his room and closed the door with a crash that raised the landlord's irritation to frenzy. For a moment it looked as if he would attack Mrs. Westerby—and then Julian and Mr. Guzzman between them turned him towards the stairs and succeeded in persuading him to go down them. Then Julian addressed his godmother.

"If I were you," he suggested quietly, "I'd leave the maid to clear up, and finish your dressing."

"*Dressing!* My dear boy, you don't realize that I didn't succeed in getting a bath."

"No tap, no water—no water, no bath," Mr. Guzzman pointed out. "Best is dress and have dinner."

"Dinner? This girl—" Mrs. Guzzman, in the doorway of her room, pointed angrily to the maid—"she cook. No tap, no water, no bath, no cook, no dinner!"

"Here—let me." Gail took over the mopping operations,

and the maid hurried downstairs. Mrs. Westerby came forward to help, but Mr. Guzzman led her to her room, pushed her inside, and closed the door.

Dinner was considerably delayed. There was nowhere to wait except on the terrace, but the sun had gone down and there was now a cold wind. Huddled in sweaters, the Guzzmans, Mark and Susie and the Cotters waited with Julian and Gail. When the landlord at last came out to announce that the meal was ready there was a cheer, and everybody but Gail and Julian surged towards the dining room.

Gail saw Mrs. Stratton and Sir Hugo coming slowly down the stairs. Julian spoke as they came out on to the terrace.

"I'm sorry about the flood," he said.

Mrs. Stratton said nothing for a moment; Sir Hugo, with rather overdone solicitude, was settling her into a chair. Then she spoke with a kind of weary contempt.

"The flood didn't matter," she said. "All I minded was the scene."

"I'm sorry about that too," Julian said.

Sir Hugo took a step closer to Julian and spoke in a low tone designed not to carry to the ears of the diners.

"Look here, Meredith, I realize that Mrs. Westerby is your godmother," he said, "and you can't very well discuss her, but . . . is she quite normal?"

"She's quite sane, if that's what you mean," Julian said angrily.

"Well, I'm sorry, but from what I've seen in the last few hours," Sir Hugo went on, "I really think there's room for doubt. Does she behave like this when she's in her own home? Or don't you know?"

"You can't blame her for the fact that the tap was faulty."

"My dear fellow," Sir Hugo said in exasperation, "that's just the point. That's just what I'm driving at. I used the tap. The Germans used the tap. Mrs. Stratton used the tap. It worked perfectly well. It was not in the least stiff."

"You're not suggesting that—"

"Yes, I am. You must really allow me to speak frankly—after all, she's ruined an expensive pair of shoes of mine, and my bedroom floor is flooded. I heard her go into the bathroom, and I'm quite certain that I heard a kind of hammering. She was in there long enough to—"

"Look," Julian broke in. "There's no point in going on with this. I don't think you really know what you're saying."

"I know exactly what I'm saying and I mean every word of it," Sir Hugo informed him. "I'm saying that there are certain types of people—not normal people—who have to make themselves the center of attention. If they feel they're getting less than their share, they do something outrageous to force people's attention back to them."

Julian looked at Mrs. Stratton.

"I'm sure you don't agree with that," he said.

She hesitated.

"I'm afraid I do," she said at last, and her tone was not friendly. "I can't believe that you don't agree with it too. I can see that you must protect her, but you're not stupid. You've got eyes, and I'm sure you use them."

"Certainly you must have seen," said Sir Hugo, "that from the moment you drove up to the village square earlier today, Mrs. Westerby has gone out of her way to pester Mrs. Stratton. Why can't she leave her alone?"

"Mrs. Stratton is her sister-in-law," Julian reminded him. "If she left her alone, it would seem far more odd than trying—as I think she's trying—to get to know Mrs. Stratton better."

Mrs. Stratton gave a faint smile.

"Mrs. Westerby and I," she said slowly, "took one another's measure many years ago. We decided that we didn't want to know one another any better. Her present behaviour is not a clumsy attempt at friendliness, but simply an effort to make me appear as ridiculous as she is. Whatever you may say, I refuse to believe that she behaves like this when she's at home. If she did, people would be justified in putting her under some kind of restraint. As soon as she saw me, she gave an effusive display of affection which I know, and I'm sure you know, she doesn't in the least feel."

"When Mrs. Stratton and I went for a walk earlier this evening," Sir Hugo said, "Mrs. Westerby joined us, gave us a detailed history of herself and assured me that now her brother was no longer here to look after Mrs. Stratton, she was determined to undertake the task herself. It really seems to me to border on a kind of persecution."

"It certainly isn't prompted by friendliness," said Mrs. Stratton in a calm, expressionless voice, "because—" She stopped. There was a long silence.

"Because what?" Julian asked at last.

"Because she hates me." Mrs. Stratton spoke quietly, but with a repressed force that frightened Gail. Before she could stop herself, she heard her own voice raised in defense of Mrs. Westerby.

"Oh no!" she protested, and saw Sir Hugo's eyes resting on her coldly. "I'm sorry—I know this is absolutely nothing to do with me, but I honestly think Julian's right, and that

Mrs. Westerby is trying to be friendly. Every time she has mentioned your name, Mrs. Stratton, she has—"

"Said something complimentary about me? I don't doubt it."

"What I do think"—Gail, to her own surprise, found herself persisting in spite of the other woman's obvious snub. "What I think is that Mrs. Westerby. . . . I mean you have a strange effect on her. I think you make her try too hard. Away from you, she's absolutely natural and . . . and likable. With you, she's completely different. I saw her at her own house, and she wasn't any different from any other rather eccentric old lady who lives alone—my grandmother, for instance. Then I saw her with you at the Flamingo, and she was . . . well, just as she is here."

"If I have this unfortunate effect on her, why can't she leave me alone?"

"Because . . . I know it's not my business, but I can't help liking her. She told me that while her brother . . . while your . . . while Mr. Stratton was alive, she hadn't succeeded in getting close to you."

"No. I saw to that."

"She wanted to leave you alone with him. She didn't want to risk being thought interfering. Now she wants to become a friend, because you both loved her brother and she feels that makes a link between you. I can see—anybody can see —how awkwardly she's going about it, but she's only trying, as Julian said, to—to—"

"Nothing Mrs. Westerby can do," Mrs. Stratton said, "will ever make us friends. I saw that as soon as I married her brother. I'm afraid he saw it too. I feel as Sir Hugo does—that she must—"

She stopped. Mrs. Westerby, in a long black dress, the beads once more about her neck, was coming out onto the terrace. She threw out her arms in a dramatic gesture.

"I am in black," she announced, "because I am a penitent. Sir Hugo"—she held out a hand—"I must hear you say that you forgive me."

Sir Hugo took the hand and bowed coldly over it; he said nothing.

"And Anita, my dear, you too? Your room, I'm happy to say, was the driest of all after my silly scrape. Let us say that all is forgotten, all forgiven."

She leaned forward and placed a kiss on Mrs. Stratton's cheek. Mrs. Stratton sat unmoving. Then she got to her feet and without a word turned to Sir Hugo. He took her hand and placed it protectively under his arm.

"Lead the way!" Mrs. Westerby commanded. "Lead the way! I have asked the landlord to do his best."

The landlord appeared, no longer red-faced and angry, but bowing and smiling and directing them to the dining room. Gail wondered how much his change of mien had cost Mrs. Westerby.

She looked at Julian as he took his place at table, and read on his face his fear of what his godmother might do or say during the meal. He need not have worried; Mrs. Westerby was at her best. She talked a good deal, but she talked well and on subjects calculated to interest her companions. She spoke of her long friendship with Julian's parents, and described her garden at Shern and her mother's old home at Chandon. Her orders to the landlord and the maid during the meal were clear, sensible and authoritative. She reminded her audience that she was in country she knew well; she told them of the excursions she had made in her youth to the high passes of the Pyrenees; she recounted anecdotes of smugglers, famous pelota players and a retired Spanish bullfighter who had come to live on the French side of the mountains. She mentioned her visits to France with her brother when they were young, and described their walks and rides about the beautiful countryside.

It was unfortunate that the meal did not end as well as it had begun. Having knitted the party together with skill and tact and even a kind of heavy charm, Mrs. Westerby at the end behaved in a manner that made Sir Hugo's diagnosis seem only too accurate.

It was his mention of a current success that brought up the subject of the theater and broke the spell that had held them all the meal. Mrs. Westerby told him that she had not seen the play—but now that he had spoken of drama, she would tell them all something she had seldom mentioned to anybody. She paused and looked round the company as though to heighten the suspense, and then leaned forward and lowered her voice. "I once—oh, a hundred years ago—I once dreamed of being a dancer!"

The diners at the other tables fell suddenly silent. An uncontrollable giggle came from Sharon Cotter.

"You *danced?*" Tag Junior's amazed, incredulous question, spoken across the room in a high squeak, made the general amusement spill over. There was a loud, prolonged burst of laughter which Mrs. Westerby, smiling and nodding, received as applause.

"I *tried* to dance," she corrected, when the gale of mirth had died down. "I know what you're all laughing at, but you mustn't suppose that I always looked as large as I do

now. I longed to be an acrobatic dancer. In my youth, I was
really very supple."

There was no more laughter; there was only acute embarrassment on every face but young Tag's. His expressed
stark disbelief.

"It was really that," Mrs. Westerby told Sir Hugo, "that
made me feel so sympathetic towards Anita from the beginning—I knew that she had worked as a designer for the theater. We had other tastes in common, too—a love of good
furniture, for example. We are going—has she told you?—
to look at some furniture in a little cottage my parents built
when they sold their house—the house is the very hotel to
which you are going, and in which you and Anita are going
to stay. We are going to look over the furniture in the cottage, and I hope she is going to let me help her to arrange
it in her house—that is, if she decides to have any of it sent
to England. I think she will. Anita—it is very good. Even
perhaps valuable—but at any rate, beautiful. My mother
would never have anything ugly near her, and I know that
you feel as she did. When you get to your house in London
—it *is* going to be in London, isn't it? I shall be able to pop
up frequently and see you. It was difficult to get down to
Cornwall, but London!" She snapped her fingers. "I can be
there in an hour. And you will be able to come down to me
for weekends. I shall insist on that, as it will do you good
to get away from town sometimes. And if Sir Hugo is
nearby, I am sure he will come to Shern too—Sir Hugo, I
should so love to show you my miniatures. One is a Samuel
Cooper—so lovely, so delicate that I can't describe it. You
must see it. You remember what Walpole said of Cooper's
work, don't you?—that it was like a life-sized Van Dyck

seen through the small end of a telescope. A *perfect* descrip-
tion. Then I have a Richard Cosway—it's exquisite, but I've
never liked it as well as the others because the ancestor of
mine whom he painted was famous for her ugliness—and he
tried to make her pretty, and in my opinion robbed her of
most of her character. But the gems are the pair painted on
lapis lazuli. These at one time belonged to my brother, but
they came to me, and they're hanging in my room today.
You must—" She stopped as her glance fell on Mrs. Stratton.

"Anita, you're tired. I've talked and talked, and look at
you—tired to death."

Gail thought the words scarcely exaggerated. Mrs. Stratton's face was the colour of the white, starched cloth that was
spread over the long table. Her eyes looked wide and fixed.

With a sudden movement, Julian pushed back his chair
and stood up.

"It's too hot in here," he said, looking across at Mrs.
Stratton. "Would you like to come out on the terrace?"

She rose without a word and moved towards him, but
Sir Hugo rose as she passed him, and took her arm and drew
her outside. Mrs. Westerby stared after them and spoke in
a regretful voice.

"I'm very, very foolish," she said, leaning confidentially
towards Gail. "I *quite* forgot that the pair of miniatures I
mentioned had belonged to my brother after his marriage—
and had been sold. I bought them—but it was devastatingly
tactless to refer to them just now without remembering
how sorry she must have been to part with them." She rose.
"Will you excuse me? I want to go to the kitchen to see
that they use my special coffee."

Julian and Gail followed her out of the room, making their way between the table at which the other diners were still seated. They wandered onto the terrace and out of the circle of light, avoiding the two silent figures—Sir Hugo and Mrs. Stratton—seated at one of the little tin tables. In the half-darkness, Gail could discern the fork of a tree; they walked up to it and she settled herself on it and addressed Julian.

"Are you going to tell me what's going on?" she asked.

"I don't know—" Julian began.

"Oh, for goodness' *sake!*" Irritation made her raise her voice. "You came out with your godmother, on your own admission to keep an eye on her. We've both sat through dinner just now watching her prove that she's just as acrobatic as she says she was when she was young. She jumped from topic to topic, and in between, she jumped on Mrs. Stratton. Why? If you say you don't know, I'll scream out loud and show you that Mrs. Westerby isn't the only one who can make a scene any time she feels like it. And don't tell me it isn't my business. It wasn't, but it is now. I've got a feeling that Mrs. Stratton needs protection."

"I've got a feeling she's getting it. Who the hell does that fellow think he is, intimating that my godmother was off her head? She's perfectly sane."

"So you keep saying. She was getting at Mrs. Stratton when she mentioned those miniatures. Why?"

"Because she thought they shouldn't have been sold, that's why."

"Not even to provide money to nurse a sick husband?"

"They had money enough when they married."

"Illness is expensive, and he was ill for a long time. And

even without illness, money can evaporate. My grandmother's did. It wasn't her fault. Her income dropped and
dropped, and the things she tried to sell—stocks—had no
sale value. If Mrs. Stratton wanted to sell her furniture and
effects, what was to stop her? They were hers—hers and her
husband's."

"They were family things. They'd been in the family for
generations. My godmother thought they shouldn't have
been sold without giving her a chance to buy them. But
nothing was ever said to her. It was only when she went
down to stay with them in Cornwall that she found out."

"Was she angry because they didn't tell her, or because
she wanted to keep them in the family, or because they
wouldn't accept money from her?"

"All three, I suppose."

"When did you get into this? You must have been fond
of her to appoint yourself—"

"I came with her because my parents asked me to. I'd be
glad if you'd stop talking about my godmother, and mind
your own business."

She spoke in a tone she strove to keep reasonable and
calm.

"Take it from my angle for a moment. I was going to
meet my brother. I was asked to make a detour and deposit
Mrs. Stratton at this cottage that my-mother-kept-when-
our-house-was-sold-it-is-now-an-hotel. I met Mrs. Stratton at
Bordeaux, and found her with an admirer in tow, which
made me feel *de trop*, which is French for two's company,
in case you don't know. Then we got stuck here, and there
was a very fishy episode relating to a scarf. Something's going on, and I'd like to know what it is, even if it isn't strictly

my business. I'm not used to undercurrents. I like everything to be out in the open—and now I'm caught up with people who all appear to be nursing dark secrets. One half of me likes Mrs. Westerby. The other half tells me she's a crazy old woman with a grievance, and so potentially dangerous. You only had to look at Mrs. Stratton's face at the dinner table just now, to know that she's getting scared too. I came out for a holiday, I don't want to get mixed up in a family feud."

"This is my holiday, too. It isn't the way I thought I'd be spending it."

She looked at his moody, worried expression, and felt a sudden uprush of sympathy.

"What were you going to do, before your parents put you on policeman duty?" she asked him.

"I was going to Scotland."

"Whereabouts?"

"The Gairloch district."

"That part of Scotland depresses me. It's sad."

"It's evocative. Which means, as you probably know, calling up spirits from the dead."

"I didn't know—but if that's it, you're right. That part of the coast is full of spirits of the dead. I'm sorry you evoked them, because you brought me back to Edward again."

"You can't always expect things to be straightforward," he pointed out. "Some facts can't be pinned down and labelled."

"I know that. But this is the first time in my life I've had to disentangle people's motives and behaviour, and I'm not enjoying it. I know that outsiders can't judge family quarrels. I'm an outsider—but you're not. You've known Mrs. Westerby all your life, and I think you're in a position to tell me what she's up to—but you won't. And what's beginning to scare me is that I think you're scared yourself. I'd rather share your fears than invent ghastly ones of my own."

"If I had any fears of the kind you mean, I'd share them," he said.

"You're honestly not frightened?"

"Of course not. I'm worried, simply because it's quite clear that my godmother and Mrs. Stratton have an unfortunate effect on one another."

"And you don't think Mrs. Stratton is scared?"

"If she is, it's because she's been listening to that blasted baronet. Are you going to let him influence you too?"

She made no reply; she was watching Mrs. Westerby on the terrace, directing the landlord to put the coffee tray on to a table. She noticed once again the easy air of command, the regal gestures, the spreading body, the large, ugly face which nevertheless, seen from this distance, could be softened and shadowed, lending credibility to the thought that once it had been handsome.

She raised her loud voice to call Gail and Julian, and they walked over to join her. Before they reached the terrace, Mrs. Stratton had risen and, without a word, gone quietly away. Mrs. Westerby stared after her in dismay.

"Without trying my beautiful coffee," she said regretfully. "Is she feeling unwell, Sir Hugo? Shall I go up to her?"

"No," he said at once. His tone was abrupt. "I should keep away if I were you. If I may speak frankly, it was your unfortunate references to the past at dinner that upset Mrs. Stratton. You have gone out of your way, it seems to me, to . . . harry her ever since you arrived."

Mrs. Westerby stared at him in the greatest astonishment. Her hand lowered the cup she was holding, and put it fumblingly on to the tray. Her voice, when she spoke, was almost quiet.

"Really, Sir Hugo. . . . May I say that I find that remark most offensive, coming as it does from one who is almost a complete stranger both to myself and to my sister-in-law?"

"Mrs. Stratton is not a person who can defend herself against the kind of . . . I might almost say persecution she has been subjected to. Therefore, I feel it—"

He stopped. Mrs. Westerby's manner had changed—and for the worse; her features had twisted themselves into a sly, knowing look—almost a leer. Her words turned him purple with fury.

"Oh dear, oh dear!" She chuckled. "Now I can see the position. Never fear, my dear Sir Hugo—I know when I am in the way. You must forgive me for having been so obtuse as to make a third where no third was welcome. You must—"

He had gone inside, striding angrily away without another word. Mrs. Westerby stood looking after him—and then she sank into a chair and, her face expressionless, glanced at Julian.

"I'm sorry," she said, almost humbly. "I'm afraid I'm making things difficult for you."

"For me?" His tone was bitter. "Not only for me. I wish to God I'd never agreed to come with you."

She said nothing. Without another glance at him or at

Gail she went slowly into the inn and up the stairs. They heard her door close.

Gail sat down suddenly; her legs were trembling. Not only her legs, she noticed with a kind of dull surprise—her hands, too. Her medical knowledge was small, but she thought this must be an evidence of her strong desire for flight. She wanted to get away—from strangers, from obscure and uneasy relationships, above all from Mrs. Westerby and Mrs. Stratton. Between the two was something that was beginning to frighten her.

She remembered Miss Teller's words of warning, and looked back with a kind of wonder at the ease with which she had allowed herself to be drawn into this situation. Refusal would have been so easy; there had been no reason on earth why she should drive Mrs. Stratton. There was money enough, Mrs. Stratton was old enough, independent enough to have arranged her journey alone. She need not have gone to lunch with Mrs. Westerby—the reason for the invitation had seemed thin then, and seemed thinner now.

She made an effort to pull herself together. One more night. Only one more night followed by a morning drive—and then she would be free.

She heard Julian speaking gently.

"Don't worry," he said. "There's nothing to worry about."

"No?"

She had meant to sound sardonic, but the monosyllable came out as a quaver.

"I shouldn't have spoken like that to my godmother," he said quietly. "It was just that I felt, for a moment, that she was a heavier responsibility than I'd bargained for."

She stared up at him.

"She . . . hates her, doesn't she?" she said. "She hates Mrs. Stratton."

Julian was so long in replying that she repeated the question angrily.

"Well, *doesn't* she? She *hates* her."

"Yes," Julian said evenly. "Yes, she does."

Chapter Seven

GAIL went to bed that night with her mind full of uneasiness. She undressed, brushed her teeth, and went through all the routine actions that were usually the preliminary to settling down to sleep, but tonight, sleep did not come.

She lay staring into the darkness, trying to make herself believe that Mrs. Westerby was nothing more than a harmless and eccentric old woman. But the evidence against this comforting solution was mounting—and the more she thought, the more certain she became that Mrs. Westerby had tied her scarf round the warning notice on purpose—why, she could not begin to guess.

She felt sorry for Mrs. Stratton—sorry was scarcely the word to express her feeling that something evil threatened her. There was something lurking behind Mrs. Westerby's unaccountable actions—but as the night wore on Gail decided that she did not, after all, want to know what it was. All she wanted was to get away. She could not go away because there was nobody to whom she could consign Mrs. Stratton.

It was almost dawn when, with a sense of relief flooding her mind, she remembered Sir Hugo.

Sir Hugo. She drew a deep breath of thankfulness. He was the obvious answer. He admired Mrs. Stratton. He had come out of his way, booked a room at the hotel in Chandon, in proof of the fact. He felt protective towards Mrs. Stratton; he had said so tonight, on the terrace.

Sir Hugo. She would go to him first thing tomorrow morning. She would seek him out, draw him aside and appeal to him frankly.

Her cares fell away. Good old Sir Hugo. In the right place at the right time. She punched the pillows and settled back contentedly, hearing the quiet exchange that would take place between them in the morning.

"Sir Hugo, could I have a word with you?"

"Certainly, Gail. What is it?"

Better to go straight to the point, even if it wasn't the real point.

"I promised to drive Mrs. Stratton to Chandon, but this holdup has made things difficult for me."

"Of course, Gail—I remember now. You were to meet your brother at San Sebastian. And this irritating delay means that you might miss him?"

"I could get a message to my brother—I know the people he's with, and I know where I could get in touch with them, but—"

"Look here; how would it be if *I* took Mrs. Stratton the rest of the way?"

"Oh . . . *would* you? Would you mind?"

"I should be delighted. But it's for her to decide. You must ask her if she would consent to the changeover from your car to mine."

"I'll do that. You're very kind, and I'm very grateful.
But . . ."

"But what?"

"I'd like to be honest with you. One of the reasons I'm
asking you to do this is because I think someone ought
to . . . well, keep an eye on Mrs. Stratton. Not on Mrs.
Stratton. On . . . on . . ."

"My dear Gail, you can say it frankly. On Mrs. Westerby.
I have been uneasy—more than uneasy. Didn't you hear
what I told her godson last night? You are doing the best
thing possible in going away. It would be madness for you
to get mixed up in any unpleasantness. You can do nothing
but what you are doing. Go away and join your brother."

"Thank you. But you—"

"My dear Gail, I shall see to it that no unpleasantness
arises. I shall drive Mrs. Stratton to Chandon. She is not
staying at Mrs. Westerby's cottage. She has a room at the
hotel, as I myself have. I shall see to it that her meetings
with Mrs. Westerby are confined to the business which has
brought them out here. You may put your mind at rest."

End of exchange. End of problem. Good old Sir Hugo.
Good . . . old . . . Sir. . . .

She awoke to the sound of loud, impatient knocks on her
door. Sleepily, she called permission to enter. The door
opened, and to her surprise she saw the landlord. He came
in, apologized for the intrusion, tested the electric switch,
found it was not working, muttered a curse, went out again
and closed the door.

She lay listening to the sounds outside. There were hurrying footsteps and muttered phrases that at first made no
sense. Then she realized that something had gone wrong

with the electric current. That meant no hot water. It also explained the non-arrival of her *café complet*.

She got up and put on a dressing gown; she had overslept and she told herself resignedly that, without doubt, someone would have hurried to the bathroom and used up whatever hot water remained. But she would go and find out.

She opened her door. At the same time, two doors opened on the opposite side of the corridor. Two men, stubble-covered, electric razors in hand, glared out at the landlord and at two youths who were fiddling with wires on the landing.

Sir Hugo spoke before Mr. Guzzman. There was no current, he shouted furiously. What had gone wrong? How was one to shave? Where was the breakfast coffee? This place was uncomfortable, so much one already knew. It was also mismanaged, understaffed and fit only for the lower order of animals.

To each item of this summary Mr. Guzzman, in the neighbouring doorway, gave an emphatic nod and a guttural sound of agreement. From the door of the bathroom, his wife shouted that the water was cold.

The landlord shouted back. His inn had been invaded—there was no other word. People—foreigners—had swarmed in without notice, without warning. Beds had to be made, food to be prepared and cooked and served, all in a hurry and all for those who had shown less than gratitude for the efforts made on their behalf. Demands and grumbles; grumbles and demands without ceasing. And now abuse. Could a man help it if for some mysterious reason the electricity had failed? It had never failed before. He had done nothing to make it go wrong. Since its installation, years before, it

had worked without trouble. And now who knew what was
the matter? One had to find out. These men were finding
out, and shouting at them would not help them to find out
any more swiftly.

He paused, purple-faced, and drew breath. And then the
door of Mrs. Westerby's room opened and she appeared
before them.

She was in the long robe she had worn during the flood
of the evening before, but on her head, this morning, was
a lace cap, ribbon-hung, which Gail had seen depicted in
very old numbers of *Punch*. She was holding a small electric kettle. On this, all eyes came to rest.

"What"—the landlord spoke with difficulty, a trembling
forefinger indicating the kettle—"what are you doing with
that?"

"Good morning. *Bon jour*." Mrs. Westerby glanced politely round the assembly, and then addressed the landlord.
"I cannot make my kettle work. It began to heat, and then
it went off."

"Ah!" The landlord drew a deep breath and glared at her
with his eyes starting from his head. "Ah! So it began to
work, and then it did not work?"

"No. It went off with a bang. It frightened me very much.
I don't think your current here is the right voltage."

"Have you been using that kettle in your room?" Sir
Hugo shouted.

"Please don't address me in that tone. Yes, I *have* been
using the kettle in my room. I invariably make my tea in the
mornings," Mrs. Westerby explained. "I've always done it.
Nothing has gone wrong before—at least, not often. Do you
mean that my using it this morning has caused some fault
in the wires?"

There was no reply from Sir Hugo, or from anybody else. Three doors banged almost simultaneously as Sir Hugo, Mr. Guzzman and Mrs. Guzzman retreated. The landlord, cursing under his breath, swept his assistants down the stairs. Mrs. Westerby was left looking at Gail.

"I don't see any reason for all that discourtesy," she said in an injured tone. "I merely attempted to make myself some tea. If the current is not right why should I be blamed? I would have thought that a man like Sir Hugo would have known better than to appear unshaven at his bedroom door and abuse a lady. I'm really surprised. No one seemed to realize that I'm the only one who didn't order coffee. I always take tea. Until my kettle worked, I could have nothing whatsoever to drink. I detest selfishness."

Gail took a long, clear look at her. The morning was clear and sunny; the sun was streaming on to the landing with an almost cruel light that showed every line, every wrinkle on the ugly, weather-beaten face. But Gail could see nothing on it but the disappointment of an entirely harmless old woman who was holding a kettle and longing for her early cup of tea.

She went to her room and washed in cold water. Dressing and packing, she pondered over the possibility of schizophrenia. She was not any too clear as to its precise meaning, but she had heard that its victims had two entirely separate codes of behaviour. Perhaps Mrs. Westerby was a schizophrenic. It was certainly easy, less frightening, to think of her in that way than in any other. She would put her theory before Sir Hugo when she spoke to him.

The electricity was working again—she had tested the light switch. Sir Hugo would by now have shaved and dressed; she would go downstairs and wait for him.

She heard the sound of a car door being slammed, and walked out on to the balcony. Looking down, she saw to her dismay that the landlord was placing Sir Hugo's luggage in his car.

Her heart began to beat faster, and she made an effort to conquer her rising panic. Perhaps he was merely having his things taken downstairs, clearing his room, paying his bill. If she went down now, she could speak to him.

She persuaded herself that she was perfectly calm, but when she reached the hall and could see, through the open front door, Sir Hugo already at his car, reaching into his pocket to tip the waiting, expectant maid, she found herself for a moment too breathless to run out and accost him. Before she could move, he had turned and caught sight of her. A look of relief overspread his face.

"Gail!"

He came towards her, and she went to meet him.

"I'm so glad to have a word with you," he said. "I've left a letter for Mrs. Stratton, as I didn't like to disturb her."

"Are you . . . are you going?"

"Yes. The road's clear."

"You're going on ahead?"

There was a pause.

"No," he said.

"I thought you were . . . I thought we were going in convoy, as we—"

"—as we did yesterday? No. Frankly, Gail—I've explained this in my letter to Mrs. Stratton—I've changed my plans. Or rather, I've decided to keep to my original plans. I've cancelled my room at the hotel. I'm not going to Chandon."

"But . . . why not?"

"Because I've come to the conclusion that my presence has a most disturbing effect on Mrs. Westerby." He spoke the name with a distaste that twisted his lips. "Whether she's off her head or not, I can't tell you. All I know is that she is violently jealous of Mrs. Stratton, and has chosen to misunderstand my purely friendly attitude. From the moment we arrived at this place, she has watched Mrs. Stratton closely, and each time that Mrs. Stratton and I have been engaged in the most casual exchange, she has forced her way into our company. Haven't you seen that?"

"Yes, but—"

"It's a most embarrassing situation, and for Mrs. Stratton's sake, I can't allow it to continue. I find Mrs. Stratton charming, and I hope I shall meet her again soon—but not when her quite impossible sister-in-law is near by. I am leaving for Mrs. Stratton's sake," he repeated with emphasis. "I won't expose her to any more of this utterly baseless and very humiliating jealousy." He took Gail's hand and pressed it. "Let us all meet one day in London. And in the meantime, *bon voyage.*"

He released her hand and got into his car. He started the engine and drove away, and Gail stood still, staring after him. She saw the car through a haze of tears—tears of rage and disappointment. Good old Sir Hugo. Good old cautious, pompous, cowardly, safety-first Sir Hugo. She herself had wanted to run away—but for her, she felt, there was some excuse; she was a girl, and she had been involved through no fault of her own; she had not, like Sir Hugo, elected to be one of the party. She didn't blame him for getting out, she told herself bitterly. All she hated him for was the manner of his flight—headlong and ungracious, with only a written message for the woman to whom he had paid such marked attention.

She was so lost in thought that Mrs. Stratton spoke before she realized that she was standing by her side.

"He's gone?" Mrs. Stratton asked quietly.

"Yes." Gail glanced at the open letter in the other woman's hand: three or four lines, no more. "He said he'd written to you."

"Yes." Mrs. Stratton raised the letter and let her hand fall again. "Yes, he wrote. He needn't have written. I heard the scene on the landing this morning, and I realized that it would prove the last straw. He already thought her out of her mind, and this morning must have convinced him."

She spoke flatly, without emphasis. A wave of sympathy swept over Gail and made her regret her plan to desert, as Sir Hugo had deserted.

"I didn't like him," was all she could find to say by way of comfort.

"I did." Mrs. Stratton spoke in the same level, toneless voice. "I did. But he was driven away, and any friends I may make in the future will be driven away too. There will be no escape. Wherever I go, she will appear—you heard her say so. She will follow me, and claim me in mock affection, and make scenes, and drag me into them, and involve me in ridicule. She . . . hates me. She *hates* me."

Gail fought against a sense of unreality. This was a golden morning in France. There was a clear road ahead, a fast car, a happy meeting with Tim and a good trip home; so much was certain. But this conversation, these words spoken quietly by a slim, quiet woman in a tone of hopelessness . . . this could not be taking place.

"Why?" she heard herself asking. "Why?"

"Because I've achieved success, and made a great deal of money, and can live in comfort—and her brother can't share any of it. She thinks he's been cheated. She feels that he should have been here to share the good things—and I feel that too. I never cease regretting that he can't enjoy them with me. But my regret is one thing, and it is natural. It's what every woman who loved her husband would feel. Hers is . . . different. Hers isn't natural. It's ugly . . . and it's dangerous. She is obsessed."

She stopped. Gail had nothing to say. With relief, she watched the approach of the American family from the house they had been occupying. She thought she had never seen anything more normal, more reassuring, more sane and wholesome than the large, loose-limbed Mr. Cotter, his calm, quiet wife and two energetic children. They paused to wait for Julian, and as he joined them, a shout from Mark Stevens indicated that he and Susie were ready to leave. The night's imprisonment was over. The road was cleared, and cars would soon pick their way along the track and roll on to the smooth, wide main road, following Sir Hugo to freedom.

Gail did not hear Mrs. Stratton leave her; only when Julian came towards her did she realize that she was alone.

"Good morning." He looked down at her unsmiling face. "Anything wrong?"

"Sir Hugo's gone."

"Early start, wasn't it? I thought he—"

"It wasn't a start. It was a finish. He pulled out. He left a note for Mrs. Stratton. She was with me just now, and

I saw it—not what was in it, just how much of it there was. A few lines."

"Did he say what he was running away from?"

"Your godmother. He seems to have had enough. She fused all the lights in the inn this morning, so nobody got baths and nobody got breakfast."

"How did she—"

"Making her morning tea. She always makes her morning tea. She wouldn't dream of—"

"All right. But I can smell coffee now—they must have got—"

"Oh yes, it's all fixed now. We'll get breakfast—all except Sir Hugo, who didn't wait. I saw him from the balcony, and came down to speak to him, but I didn't get a chance. All I got to do was listen, and say goodbye."

"And I suppose he went before you could persuade him to stay and support you—is that it?"

"That's it."

"What were you going to ask him?"

"To take over Mrs. Stratton—what else?"

"And what were you going to do?"

"Go away. Go back to people I understand. Go on to San Sebastian and Tim and all those naval men you dislike so much. Like you, I took on more than I bargained for. You can't get out of it—but I thought I could. And if you're opening your mouth to say that your godmother's a lovable old dear, and as harmless as a kitten, save it."

He made no answer. He left her and went to the door of the inn and spoke to the landlord, and presently the smell of coffee came nearer and a large tin tray was placed on a table nearby.

"Come on," Julian said. "Breakfast. Get some coffee and croissants inside you, and you'll feel better."

The coffee was superb, the croissants were hot and crisp; they tore them apart and ate them dripping with butter. Gail poured coffee and hot milk into huge, red-and-blue-checked Basque cups, and they cradled them in their hands and drew in hot, satisfying gulps.

"Feeling better?" Julian asked at last.

"Yes, thank you."

"Were you really contemplating running away, like the gallant Sir Hugo?"

"Yes. I thought it over in the night, and decided it wasn't my business, and that Sir Hugo would be delighted to act as escort to Mrs. Stratton. After all, he'd been giving a convincing exhibition of an enamoured man. But he vanished. He said he'd pick up the threads again when he could get Mrs. Stratton alone. But Mrs. Stratton is certain that she never will be, from now on."

He helped her to place the luggage in her car, and stood looking down at her.

"Do you really believe," he asked slowly, "that my godmother could harm anybody?"

Gail looked at Mrs. Stratton, who was walking towards them.

"She's done some harm," she said. "Hasn't she?"

He opened the car door for Mrs. Stratton and settled her into her seat. There was no sign of Mrs. Westerby.

"You'd better go on ahead," Julian said. "We'll pass you on the road. We've got to get to the cottage first to see it's opened up."

He stood watching the car drive away and Gail gave her

attention to the hazards of the road. Huge blocks of stone
had been cleared to one side to allow passage back to the
main road; a workman flagged them on, and soon Gail put
on speed and felt thankfully the smooth surface under the
wheels.

Beside her, Mrs. Stratton sat in silence, staring straight
ahead. As always, her face betrayed nothing, but Gail knew
that she must be thinking of Sir Hugo's humiliating with-
drawal. Once more, pity filled her—but it was not strong
enough to keep back another feeling that had been growing
in her since the effects of the coffee had worn off. She knew,
to her chagrin, that her uneasiness was returning; she realized that she had slowed down and was giving anxious
glances in the mirror to see if Julian's car was in sight. She
wanted him to pass—and then she was determined to keep
close behind. He gave her a sense of safety.

Mrs. Stratton spoke suddenly. There was something in
her tone that Gail could not identify.

"You don't have to go on, you know," she said. "If you
feel you want to turn back, all you have to do is say so, and
we'll turn back."

"It's entirely up to you," Gail said. "If it's only a matter
of furniture—"

"Not 'only' furniture. I felt it was a chance to get something of my husband's. Everything we had was sold while
he was ill. I felt he'd like me to have the furniture in the
cottage. But things haven't been very pleasant for you, and
I have no right to ask you to go on if you don't want to."

If she would only shout, Gail thought, it would be a relief; it was frightening to feel the force and the tenseness

behind the words, and to contrast them with the calm, level voice.

The mountains were close and high and enclosing. Gail felt as though she was driving into a fastness from which escape would be impossible. There was no traffic; the road twisted, higher and higher; the few houses in sight seemed to cling to the slopes like climbers whose numb fingers would soon loose their hold, sending them crashing down to the dark, shadowed, sinister valley.

"If you want to go back, we'll go," she heard Mrs. Stratton saying again.

"We'll go on," Gail said.

"Very well." Mrs. Stratton spoke quietly, but Gail was at last able to identify the note in her voice. It was desperation.

Chapter Eight

THE first glimpse of the cottage, which by now Gail had heard so much about, brought her back swiftly to a sense of normality.

She had not had a picture of it in her mind. She had not even troubled to guess at its size; cottages, she was aware, varied as widely as the people who owned them, and might be large houses set in lawns, or modest dwellings lining a village street.

But this, she felt at once on seeing it, was a real cottage: a small country residence surrounded by magnificent scenery. Built in the Basque style, it had green shutters newly painted, and rose-pink walls.

It had not been difficult to find; she had simply followed Julian. He had passed her and then led her, slowing down and waiting for her at confusing crossroads to make certain that she did not miss the way.

The first sight of habitation, after a long spell of mountains and cattle, had been the main house, now the hotel. It was built on a promontory overlooking a view breathtakingly beautiful, but had a vaguely mournful look, like a dog whose owners had gone away. Julian had not stopped; he

took the lakeside track that skirted the hotel; it was a narrow, rutted road, winding through woods and affording occasional glimpses of the wind-ruffled water.

When they drew up at the cottage, Mrs. Stratton sat
looking at it, saying nothing. The ancient man and wife
who acted as caretakers came to take out the luggage; they
transferred Mrs. Stratton's cases to Julian's car.

"You mustn't hurry away, Anita," Mrs. Westerby said,
appearing round the side of the house. "You must come in
and look over the cottage—though of course you can do that
as often as you care to, later on. Gail, there is to be no question of your leaving until tomorrow. You are going to stay
with me tonight, and when you go away tomorrow, Julian
is going to follow you and see you safely on your way."

"There's no need—" Gail began.

"I'm taking you as far as the frontier," Julian said, coming out of the house and joining them.

"I can get to the frontier by myself."

"I daresay you can," he said. "But I need some sherry,
and I shall hop across the border and buy some cheap."

"My dear boy," Mrs. Westerby protested, "the people in
these mountains have been hopping over the border, as you
term it, since time immemorial. They are still doing it. All
you have to do is name what you want; if it's French, they
will have it, if it's Spanish, they will get it for you. I daresay
some of those young contrabandistas I knew are still alive;
if not, their sons will be following in their footsteps. Why
would my mother have been able to sell that great house so
easily if the hoteliers who bought it hadn't been assured of
a steady, cheap supply of everything they wanted?"

Julian laughed and Gail, studying him, saw that he was

enjoying her own sense of release. There was nothing in this atmosphere to recall the discomfort and uneasiness of the previous night. The sun was warm, the air bracing; the caretakers were all smiles and Mrs. Westerby reassuringly normal.

Mrs. Stratton, Gail and Julian went indoors and followed her slowly round the rooms of the cottage.

"You can see now why my mother couldn't bear to give it up," she said. "When you get to the hotel, Anita, you'll see a number of pieces, among the furniture there, that belonged to my mother—but nothing they have there can compare with what you see here."

They were standing in the little square drawing room; its windows faced south and west and lighted a room that might never have been without an occupant; the floors and the furniture were brightly polished, the ornaments were in place, beautifully-bound books stood in perfect order. It did not need a connoisseur to judge the beauty and value of the furniture.

"Edward often wrote letters at that desk," Mrs. Westerby told them. "He moved it so that he could see the view better. 'How can you write and gaze out at the view at one and the same time?' I used to ask him—I liked the desk better where it was, but he never moved it back again."

Julian had picked up a delicate porcelain figure and was examining it.

"Vincennes," Mrs. Westerby said promptly. "That little figure is 1753—you know, of course, that Louis XV gave a royal concession to the factory for making porcelain?"

"I didn't think his mind ran on porcelain figures," Julian commented. "What would happen to all this"—he waved a hand that embraced the cottage and its surroundings—"if the caretakers died?"

"Their sons and daughters would step into their place," Mrs. Westerby stated confidently. "My mother's family lived in the big house for generations. As you can see for yourselves, they were the focal point of all life here. There was no village, only scattered little houses whose owners made a living by smuggling. Some of them still do—but from the time my forebears settled here, they made themselves responsible for the welfare of every person who worked for them or who lived within reach of their care. The cottage means, today, what the big house used to mean in the old days. I hope Anita will use it very often in the future."

It was clear to Gail, and she thought it must be especially clear to Mrs. Stratton too, that if the cottage was stripped of its contents, it would lose its personality and its purpose. But the furniture was Edward's; he was dead, and his widow had come to claim what was hers, and she would have it packed up and sent away. It would be the end.

It would be a pity, Gail thought, if she wanted the furniture, and wondered what Mrs. Westerby was thinking.

Mrs. Westerby's face was very pale, but she was quieter, more restrained, more dignified than Gail had ever seen her. She seemed to be struggling to say something; as they watched her, she turned to Mrs. Stratton and spoke in a tone almost humble.

"Well, here it is, Anita. I wish that you had come out alone—but you didn't want to take possession of the things unless I came too—so here I am. I would have liked you to accept the cottage, but perhaps it was asking too much to

expect you to see our family as we did. It was certainly asking too much, I know, to expect you to immure yourself
here—except for short visits. If I had been younger, if I had
been a person nearer to you in age, I might perhaps have
begged you to consider some kind of joint residence here—
my cottage and Edward's furniture, and everything and
everybody round us full of memories of him. But I do not
think you would have cared for that."

Mrs. Stratton had been gazing out of the window. She
turned slowly, and the eyes of the two women met. Gail
could read nothing in the expression of either, but she saw
the colour leave Mrs. Westerby's cheeks.

"No." Mrs. Westerby answered herself. "No, it wouldn't
have been possible. If you couldn't endure me while Edward was alive—and I don't in any way blame you, because
I know that I'm thought troublesome and eccentric—if you
couldn't put up with me then, how much less can you have
patience with me now that he's dead."

Still Mrs. Stratton said nothing. After a pause, Mrs. Westerby continued on a brisker note.

"Well, my hope is to see a good deal of you in London.
You must let me help you to settle in your new home. You
must come down to Shern to meet my friends, and I must
go up to London to meet yours. There is a link between us,
and we must not let it break. And now, shall we go and
look at the garden, and at the lake? We'll take the lake walk
first, before the clouds come out and spoil the nice sunshine
—the water looks so much prettier when it's sparkling."

She went on, taking the lead and talking to the others
over her shoulder as they followed her along a narrow,

paved path. "This is the way to the little belvedere my
mother built. Look!"

They went into a little glass-enclosed shelter which had
cushioned seats placed before the windows, and gazed out
over the spreading view.

"This was her favourite spot by day," Mrs. Westerby
said, "and Edward's too. He tried to get the view down on
canvas—you've got one of his paintings of it, haven't you,
Anita?—but he wasn't pleased with the results. He said he
couldn't reproduce the full variety of the colours. And now
I'll take you to the walk we all loved. Up this way—it's
rather steep."

They toiled up a grassy incline; it was very short, and at
the top Julian, who had given Mrs. Stratton a hand to aid
her, gave a startled exclamation and a sharp warning.

"Watch out!"

"There's no need to sound so alarmed, my dear boy."
Mrs. Westerby sounded indulgent. "It's just the momentary
feeling of stepping into space, that's all. As you see, there's
a perfectly good, wide bank to stand on."

Gail, at Julian's exclamation, had clambered up the last
foot or two with caution, but even so it was a shock to find
the slope terminating abruptly and levelling out to a narrow
shelf that dropped sheerly away to the lake below. She took
a gingerly step forward, glanced over the edge and stepped
back hastily.

"Now, that's something we never did as children," Mrs.
Westerby told her. "My father always did the same thing
to any children who came to stay with us—gave them a
warning and told them, with no attempt at disguise and
with no merciful skipping of nasty details, what would hap-

pen to them if they walked near the edge. There's no danger of crumbling—the ground is quite firm—but he considered it essential to give children a sense of danger. 'Show them the penalties' he used to say, 'and they'll heed the warnings.' He would have deplored that great, ugly, defacing wire fencing that was put up when the big house became an hotel. He would have considered it unnecessary."

"Without that great, ugly, defacing fencing," Julian pointed out, "most of the guests would fall into the lake before they'd paid their bills."

"Nonsense, my dear boy." Mrs. Westerby threw the words over her shoulder; she was leading them along the track. "Nonsense! You can't hedge people round with protective barriers."

"But children—" began Gail.

"Children on farms have to learn to keep out of the bull's way," Mrs. Westerby pointed out in her most decided tones. "Do you think Swiss or Austrian children grow up with hideous wire fencing stuck up on every ski slope? Accidents, my father used to say, occurred only when children were not told *exactly* what the danger was and *exactly* what would happen to them if they didn't obey warnings to avoid it. I used to run along this edge quite alone, as a very small child, and when he was old enough, Edward used to do the same. We didn't have to have nurses screaming behind us. We *knew*. At the hotel, where fools doubtless stay sometimes, perhaps there has to be some kind of warning— but people can read. A notice in several languages would have been quite as efficacious, and far less ugly than that monstrous wire. Now!" She rounded a corner, waited for them, and then threw out a hand. "Here it is!" she exclaimed.

"Our most beloved, most private, most time-honoured re-treat."

The path had widened into a semicircle on which they could stand and gaze at a magnificent panorama. A few large boulders made natural seats, and on one of them Mrs. Westerby sat, looking out over the water.

"We called this spot the Moonlight Watch," she said. "When there was a moon in summer, we used to come out here—accompanied, as children, because the moon might go behind clouds and leave us with no light to guide us. We would come and sit here—quietly. I say quietly, because even now, as you can hear, my voice is an intrusion. At night, with the moon shining on the lake, there is such peace here that one would hardly venture to speak. Peace enwraps you on this spot. You might be in space. You would think you were on the moon itself if you couldn't see it shining above you and, in reflection, below you too. Isn't it quite, quite perfect?"

She fell silent, and they could test the truth of her words. She had scarcely exaggerated. The place had an almost un-earthly stillness.

Gail, looking downwards, gave a shiver.

"I wouldn't like to swim in that water," she said.

"*Swim?* My dear girl, you couldn't *swim* in this lake!" Mrs. Westerby protested. "It's far too dangerous!"

"What's dangerous about it?" Julian asked. "Cramp from the cold? No whirlpools that I can see."

"Rocks. Nasty rocks like rows of teeth. My father kept on his study desk a double row of jagged wooden points, just like the jaw of a crocodile. He used to open it"—Mrs. Westerby put her wrists together and drew apart the palms

of her hands—"wide, like this, and then suddenly—" She
brought her palms sharply together with a slap. "Scrunch!
just like that. 'If *that's* what you want to happen to you,'
he told us, 'then try to swim in the lake. Better still, or
worse still, jump into it.'"

Mrs. Stratton was turning back; it was time, she said, for
her to go over to the hotel.

"Then Julian will take you," Mrs. Westerby said, bringing up the rear as they walked back in single file along the
path. "But if any of you want to find me at any time, this is
where I shall be—breathing in the peace of this lovely spot.
If there are ghosts, this is where the ghosts of my family
would walk. And nobody would mind them a bit, because
they would just be strolling, as we are now, and as they did
when they were alive—contented and at peace. Gail, why
don't you go with the others and look at the hotel?"

Gail thought it would be a good idea, and drove to it
with Mrs. Stratton and Julian. She found that the interior
of the house had retained some of its homelike atmosphere;
no attempt had been made to change the large, square entrance hall; a low screen placed round a table was the only
sign of a reception desk.

Mrs. Stratton and her luggage were taken up to her room.
She would not, she told Gail and Julian, ask them to stay
to lunch; to invite them would mean inviting Mrs. Westerby and this—she spoke for the first time openly and without reserve—she said she would not do.

"I'm sorry to sound unkind," she said, "but . . . perhaps
there are too many memories here. I don't know . . . all I
know is that I feel a little upset—I cannot bear any more
of your godmother for the present, Julian."

"I quite understand," he said. "Just as long as you remember that she means well."

She smiled—a faint, entirely incredulous smile.

"Don't let's pretend any more," she begged. "I'm here, safe at the hotel. I shall have to say goodbye to Gail before she goes, but I hope she will come and say goodbye to me here."

Julian and Gail watched her going out of sight in the lift; then they turned and walked towards the door. Gail saw Julian pause and then turn back to say something to a clerk sitting at the desk. She did not hear his question, but she heard the man's answer: The gentleman was out, he said, but he had left a message. She saw Julian take the folded paper; he read it, crumpled it and dropped it into the wastepaper basket.

When he rejoined Gail, she glanced at him enquiringly.

"Someone you know staying here?" she asked in surprise.

"Yes. I wasn't quite sure when he was arriving."

He said no more, and she was annoyed at having shown any curiosity. Also, she found, getting into his car and watching him take his place at the wheel, she was vaguely uneasy. She didn't want to know anything he didn't want to tell her, she told herself irritably, but it was odd that he should have said nothing whatsoever, up to this moment, of having a friend staying here. This hotel wasn't at Brighton or Palm Beach; it was stuck on a mountain on the edge of the Pyrenees, where the arrival of an acquaintance or—even more, a friend—was a matter either of singular coincidence, or prearrangement; in either case, it would surely have been natural for him to have said that he expected to see someone he knew. A devil of perversity seized her.

"Don't you want to speak to him?" she asked.

"Speak to whom?"

"Your friend."

"What friend?" He sounded genuinely surprised.

"The one you asked the hotel clerk about."

He frowned. "I'd rather you didn't mention the incident to my godmother," he said, "or to Mrs. Stratton."

The last remnants of patience slipped from her. She spoke in a voice that shook with fury.

"Look," she said, "there's been enough mystery on this trip. I don't care who your friend is or what he's doing here, but I'm not going to creep about sharing secrets with you or with anybody else. Early tomorrow morning, thank goodness, I'll be on my way. In the meantime, I'll do my best to get over my feeling of sitting on a time bomb that might go off any minute and take me with it. All I hope is that it doesn't go off before I do. I don't mind facing things in the normal way—that is, I can run my own life and take what comes—but nobody had any business to include me in this setup. Especially you. You knew before we set out that we were going to have trouble, and I'll bet you could guess what sort of trouble it was going to be. I never did you any harm, and I think you played a mean trick in letting me get tied up in this circus without giving me any kind of warning. I'm prepared to go through a lot for my own family, but I can't see why I should—"

"Oh, for God's sake, shut up!" he shouted.

He need not have asked; she had run out of breath. She drew in a fresh supply, and noted through her anger that the car had stopped. They were somewhere halfway between the hotel and the cottage. She saw Julian put out a hand and switch off the engine.

"If you're fed up," he said, turning on her, "what the hell do you think *I* am?"

"Who the hell cares? She's your godmother—not mine."

"What do you propose I should have done when Mrs. Stratton talked you into driving her here? Sent an anonymous letter of warning? Asked you to meet me, and hinted vaguely about crying off? Hints—to you? You would have asked me for a printed list of all possible risks, signed with my full name. Hints? You wouldn't recognize a hint if I threw it in your face. All you want, all you've wanted since you got to that village yesterday, is a clear analysis of a situation which hasn't even developed. How could I warn you not to come? Haven't you realized yet that I didn't know what was coming?"

"That's not true. You told me you came out to keep an eye on your godmother."

"So I did. If you keep an eye out for possible trouble, does that necessarily mean it's bound to come? Can't something be put down to my having exaggerated the risks? If I felt uneasy, was I justified in making you uneasy too—on nothing but my own apprehensions? Before I set out on this trip, remember that I had never once seen my godmother and Mrs. Stratton together. In fact, I'd never seen Mrs. Stratton at all. How could I foresee what tension, if any, would build up between them? The reason for my godmother's journey was a perfectly valid one—how valid, you saw for yourself in the cottage a short time ago. One of them owned the house and the other owned the contents, and one of them seemed to think she couldn't act without the other being present. And so they arranged a date that would suit them both, and Mrs. Stratton took elaborate precautions to avoid meeting us on the way."

"And your godmother took elaborate precautions to hole us all up at that inn. You knew perfectly well she draped her scarf round that notice and tampered with the directional arrow. You should have come out into the open and dealt with her, because she's dangerous. But instead of restraining her, you acted as though—"

"Don't you," he broke in, "ever think of anybody but yourself? Just because you scare so easily, do I have to—?"

"Easily? You saw what happened last night, didn't you? You saw Mrs. Stratton's face? How far do things have to go before you forget you're a godson and remember that you're in charge of a woman who acts like—"

"For God's sake," he ground out, "what harm do you imagine a poor old unhappy woman can do you?"

"I'm not thinking of myself. I'm thinking of Mrs. Stratton."

"You weren't thinking of Mrs. Stratton early this morning. Sir Hugo just raced you to the exit. When you saw what a stinking figure he made running out, you decided to stick it out. If you want to get your things and move over to the hotel now, then do. Nobody'll stop you."

"I'll stay at the cottage. I don't think Mrs. Westerby is quite right in the head and you don't think so either, but—" She stopped, struck by a sudden shaft of enlightenment. "That man!" she exclaimed.

"What man?"

"The man at the hotel. The man you know. He's a doctor, isn't he?"

"He's nothing of the kind."

"But you knew he was coming. You must have arranged
. . . *did* you arrange for him to be at the hotel?"

"No, I didn't. It was his idea."

"Then I'm right. He's a psychiatrist."

"He is not."

She scarcely heard him; she was following her own line
of thought.

"You expected to have trouble with Mrs. Westerby, and
you undertook to keep an eye on her on the way out here,
but you either arranged for reinforcements to be here, or
you sent for them. Which?"

He stared at her frowning, intent face and seemed to
make up his mind.

"If I tell you," he asked slowly, "can you keep your
mouth shut?"

"I won't make any trouble, if that's what you mean? You
don't want his presence known, as they say in books?"

"Not yet."

"All right. Who is he?"

The answer was so totally unexpected that it took her
breath away.

"He's my father," Julian said.

"Your . . . your father?" she said stupidly at last.

"Yes."

"You sent for him?"

"He wanted to come himself. I told him that I'd come
out with her, and if on the way I came to the conclusion
that I needed him, I'd get in touch with him."

"So you . . . got in touch?"

"Yes."

"When?"

"Yesterday, at that village. Just before dinner. I telephoned to his hotel in Paris."

"And . . . and asked him to come?"

"Yes. He'd booked a room provisionally at the Chandon hotel. He only had to confirm it."

"And he's here, and you don't want her to know?"

"It's absolutely essential"—the gravity in his voice made her shiver—"it's absolutely essential that you should keep what I've told you to yourself."

"Because the sight of her . . . her psychiatrist suddenly appearing would . . . would touch her off?"

"Will you stop being melodramatic? I've told you already—my father is not a psychiatrist. He's—"

He stopped abruptly.

"*What* is he?" Gail shouted in fury. "Go on—tell me. What is he?"

"He is—he was—attached to the C.I.D."

When at last she found her voice, it sounded like someone else's; someone who suffered from a terrified stammer.

"S-S-Scotland Yard?" she managed at last.

She saw the anger and exasperation drain out of his face. Something in her defenseless look touched him; perhaps he saw, for the first time, the extent of her involvement. His voice, when he spoke, was firm, but very gentle.

"He is an old friend of Blanche's," he said slowly. "He loves her. He and my mother are her oldest, her greatest—sometimes I think her only—friends. He has come out here to help her—that's all. The message he left at the desk was to tell me that it would be better not to mention his arrival until he had had an opportunity of talking to me—alone. So I asked you to say nothing. Now do you feel better?"

She tried to say that she felt much worse; instead, the strange voice asked a strange question.

"If he's from the C.I.D., if he came out here because you sent for him, then he must believe that there's some kind of . . . of serious trouble."

Julian took her hand and held it and spoke firmly.

"He is here," he said, "simply to ensure that no trouble occurs."

Chapter Nine

GAIL had lunch at the cottage with Julian and Mrs. Westerby. The food was well-cooked and well-served—but she could not eat it. She wanted desperately to be quiet, to think; if Julian's eyes had not been on her, anxious and—she thought—apprehensive, she would have left the table and gone up to her bedroom and locked herself in. Her mind was in confusion and each moment in Mrs. Westerby's presence made the confusion worse.

The small, shrewd eyes came to rest on her at last, and Mrs. Westerby spoke with motherly solicitude.

"Gail, you're looking very white—and you're not eating. Have you got a headache?"

Gail grasped the lifeline.

"Yes. Yes, I have. Would you mind if I went upstairs to lie down for a little while?"

"Mind? My dear child, I'm a selfish monster for not having seen how exhausted you were. All those miles of driving, half of them over mountainous roads—and here I've been talking about the old days and failing in my duty as a hostess. Would you like me to go up with you?"

"No. Oh no," Gail said with more haste than tact. "I'll just rest for a little while."

"Have you got aspirins?"

"Yes, thank you."

"I've got a special headache mixture which I make up myself. Julian shall take it up to you," Mrs. Westerby promised.

When Julian knocked, she was lying on the bed as she had thrown herself down, hands crossed behind her head, her eyes closed. He came in with a glass half-filled with a cloudy white liquid. She opened her eyes and looked at it with a face screwed up in distaste.

"What's that?" she asked.

He sat down on the edge of the bed, looking at her with a half-smile.

"Poison," he said, putting the glass on the table. "Didn't you hear? She makes it up herself. You drink it down and that's the end of you."

"If you think talking like that is going to make me feel any better—"

"If this doesn't finish you off, she's instructed me to carry you to the Moonlight Watch and cast you down on to the rocks below." He opened his hands and snapped them shut in imitation of Mrs. Westerby's crocodile-jaw action. "And now that you know the worst, how about pulling yourself together and getting up and coming for a long walk with me to cure this attack of liver, caused by driving too long without proper exercise?"

"All I want is to be left alone."

"To brood?"

"To clear my head. It's going round."

"It shouldn't be going round. You've overwound it. The only way to cure your malady is to clear your mind of all the rubbish that's accumulated there during the past few hours. You've cluttered up your brain with a lot of highly seasoned and entirely erroneous ideas. If you'll close your eyes and relax completely, I shall help you to throw out the debris."

She closed her eyes and wished it were as easy to close her mind. Julian's voice seemed to come from far away.

"My godmother," he said, "is old, and lonely, and unhappy. She lived for years with a beloved brother. When he married, she had a store of affection which she longed to pour out on his wife and even perhaps—though this wasn't likely—on his children.

"You've seen Mrs. Stratton. She is good-looking, charming in a quiet, rather delicate way, and she has taste and experience and a love of beautiful things . . . and beautiful people. The first meeting with her sister-in-law must have been an unpleasant shock to them both. There was no common ground after all—and Blanche's dreams were at an end. From then on, there was no place for her in her brother's life.

"But she loved him, and she was afraid of losing him, and so she kept trying. And the harder she tried, of course, the more oddly she behaved and the more Mrs. Stratton withdrew—and then Blanche went too far, and defeated her own ends. And then Mrs. Stratton became rich, and remembered a cottage in France, in which she owned some furniture that was probably very valuable and that would look well in the nice new house she was proposing to buy. And she arranged to come out and meet Blanche here.

"Blanche had been in a bad state of nerves ever since Edward's death. My mother thought that this visit would turn her mind from the past to the future. I didn't agree—but I came along as driver to one part of the expedition. To you, my godmother is an ugly, awkward old woman with a loud voice—to my parents, she's an old and valued friend. To me, she's a warmhearted, open-handed, affectionate, amusing and entirely lovable godmother. I love her —it's as simple as that. I wouldn't have come out here with her if I hadn't loved her, and if I hadn't . . . trusted her."

He stopped. Gail spoke without opening her eyes.

"You mean that even though you're here to be a sort of watchdog, and your father's here to be a second watchdog, you trust her not to make trouble?"

"Quite so. But it didn't occur to me—until we talked in the car before lunch—that the affair would look so very different from your angle. If it had occurred to me, I would have talked to you frankly at the very beginning."

She opened her eyes.

"When was the very beginning?"

"The evening I drove you back to town from your brother-in-law's farm. I think I would have said something then—but you said that you liked Blanche and so I decided to leave it. I thought you'd got beyond her odd exterior, got to understand her somehow—but I was wrong. You liked her simply because she had behaved normally. When she gave signs of being not so normal, you were quite ready to believe she was crazy. And so she was, to misread maps on our way down to Bordeaux, to delay me so that we'd be round about there when you and Mrs. Stratton arrived. She was crazy when she gave way to an impulse and tampered with those signs and got us all caught in the inn. So I can't really blame you for imagining things. If I hadn't known

Blanche so well and so long, I might have imagined things too. I had an advantage. You didn't know her at all, and so you had a bad night and decided to give up. And my father's arrival was the last straw. I hoped it would make you feel safe—but I can see it didn't. You now imagine the very worst. And I don't suppose anything I've been saying now has had any effect whatsoever."

"If you mean do I feel more in the picture—"

"Well?"

"Then no. I don't. But I never wanted to be. You told me to mind my own business, and that's just what I was trying to do when I decided to get out and let Sir Hugo have Mrs. Stratton to himself. He got out first—and the reasons for his going weren't the ones he stated in his farewell note. He thought there was something fishy and he didn't bother to stop and find out what it was. It sounds silly to say he was scared, but he was. And so would I be now, in spite of all your speeches, if—"

He waited.

"If what?"

"If you weren't here."

"I'm glad to hear you say so. Would any other man give you the same feeling of confidence, or do I have some special merit as a bodyguard?"

"You're bigger than most," Gail smiled.

"Anything else?"

"You don't fuss much. You're quiet and sort of steady."

"Big, unfussy, quiet, steady. What other qualities do you look out for in a man?"

"Rather more response to feminine attraction than you've shown to date."

"You can't get response from a big, unfussy, quiet, steady man until he's had a chance to size up the attraction."

She was genuinely surprised.

"You mean it didn't hit you straight off?"

"Not too hard." He smiled. "There are so many pretty girls. You meet them everywhere. There has to be a good deal more."

"There is. Can't you see?"

"I was talking about inner qualities."

"Such as?"

"Gentleness and kindness and tenderness and faithfulness."

"You ought to meet our Miss Teller, who's bringing out a dictionary of out-of-date words. Did that date you missed have all those—what was the word?—qualities?"

"She was only for an evening."

"I see. You're on the lookout for ever and ever?"

"Aren't you?"

"Not exactly on the lookout. Once I marry a man, I'll see to it that it's for ever and ever."

"It won't be unless you employ the method you were using just now—making certain that the basic structure is solid. What's the use of charm and looks if they're not based on bigness and quietness and unfussiness and steadiness? That's stage one. Once you've got the solid qualities, you can—"

"Can what?"

"You can go ahead with confidence. Like this." He moved closer and gathered her to him and held her. "This is stage two."

He kissed her. She was so unresponsive that he released her and held her away from him to read her expression.

"Well?" he asked.

"Don't go away," she begged. "Hold me—please."

He held her once more, but when he sought her lips, she drew away.

"No, don't kiss me again—not yet. Not till my head's cleared."

"What's your head got to do with it?"

"It's going round.—How did this start?"

"It's been going on since we met. We've just identified it, that's all. Now can I kiss you?"

She gave a happy sigh.

"Yes. And then tell me about stage three."

They had left Mrs. Westerby's headache remedy untouched on the table, and gone out for what Julian called real exercise.

But even real exercise, scrambling up precipitous slopes and sliding down again, did not restore them to calm. They came back to the cottage hand in hand, and Gail went up to her room to change; instead she sat at the window, gazing out at the view but seeing only a rapturous future which began with a month's notice to the Beetham Brothers.

When she went downstairs for dinner, she found nobody in the drawing room. Julian's car was no longer parked beside her own on the drive, but after ten minutes spent in gazing out of the window wondering miserably where he had gone, she heard him returning. A short while later, he walked into the room holding an armful of bottles. Before putting them down, he bent and laid a long kiss on her lips.

"Went over to the hotel for drinks," he explained. "Must lay in a stock for celebration." He glanced round. "Blanche not down?"

"Not yet."

"What'll you drink?"

He was pouring it out when the caretaker's wife came in to say that Madame begged to be excused; she was tired and wished to stay in her room.

A slight crease of worry appeared on Julian's forehead. He put down the glasses.

"I'll go up and see her," he said.

After a short interval, he returned, and Gail saw that he was looking satisfied.

"She just wants to be quiet," he announced. "She doesn't want to go to bed. She's going to have a light meal in her room and then she thinks she might take a short stroll along the ghost walk."

"Let's go with her. Did you say anything—"

"About us? No. It didn't seem a good moment. I tried to see my father while I was at the hotel, but he'd gone out—to do a bit of climbing, they said. At his age! I'll go over when we've eaten, and have a chat with him and bring him back here—then he can meet you, and we'll spring the news. What time do you want to start in the morning?"

"Dawn."

"Dawn?"

"Dawn. And dawn, in my family, means dawn and not yawning and saying it's absurd to start so early."

"Don't imagine I'm thinking of myself. Not for a minute. I'm merely wondering if the staff will be—"

"We don't stop for coffee. We have it on the way. I

think breakfast on the way is much more fun. You'll see."

"All right. Dawn it is," he said without enthusiasm. "Shall I order a picnic lunch?"

"No. I will. You'll ask for pâté and all the rest of it. All we want is bread and cheese and a bottle of wine."

"A dawn start without coffee, and bread and cheese. The March of the Spartans. I'm going to enjoy being married to you." He paused and spoke in a more serious tone. "I'm glad you're going. I'm glad you're getting back to base. We shouldn't have let you come. If I haven't said thank you, take it as read."

The caretaker's wife opened the door and announced that dinner was ready. They followed her into the dining room.

"Fish soufflé, veal hammered out for frying, and green salad," Julian said as they went.

"How do you know?"

"I came in through the kitchen. I wanted to choose the wine."

There was not much conversation during the meal. Julian was content to combine the twin pleasures of eating and gazing at her, and Gail was in a silent mood. Now that the time for leaving had come, she could look back with surprise and shame at the fears she had entertained—and exhibited. It was humiliating to discover that she had less poise than she had claimed. She had always assumed that she would keep her head in any emergency; there had been no emergency, but she had come near to losing her head.

"Are you brooding again?" Julian asked.

"Yes. I've discovered I'm not the intrepid type I prided myself on being. When I look back on all this, the only hope I'll have of boosting my pride is to remember that you went through some pretty uneasy moments too."

"But then, I never set myself up as a hero," he pointed out. "I could give you a list of my phobias, beginning with fast drivers, steep ski slopes, rearing horses, oversexed women and flying cockroaches."

"Not a bad beginning. Go on."

"Heights above the fourteenth floor, society Mums, Customs officials and men wearing nylon masks over their faces. And going off the high diving board."

"Why go off it?"

"That sneaking fear that if you don't conquer it, it'll conquer you. I've never believed that, and I shall never instill it into our children—but it was instilled into me, and I can never instill it out again. I might try that method Blanche was telling us about—telling our children what to expect if they don't read the warning notices."

It was a strangely quiet end, she reflected, to a singularly eventful journey. She would remember all her life this small, candlelit room, this gleaming oval table with crystal and silver set upon it and Julian seated opposite, his eyes on hers.

"I'm looking forward to meeting Tim," he remarked.

"But you don't like service people; they make you feel old, and they talk a nasty common language."

"I said that?"

"Yes."

Julian, watching her, saw her becoming more serious.

"How much are you going to tell your father about the trip?" she asked.

"Everything."

"Julian—"

"Well?"

"Why *did* she tamper with that warning notice? Haven't you ever asked her?"

"No, not straight out. You heard her explanation. I was sure she'd stick to it. But what she wouldn't tell me, she'll tell my father. When I said I'd bitten off more than I could chew, it was an understatement. I was the wrong person to bring her out. I hadn't any authority, any old-friend privileges to count on. My father has. Thank God he's here."

They did not have coffee; Gail did not want any, and Julian decided to have it at the hotel with his father. They parted at the foot of the stairs and he watched her go up to finish her packing. She turned to utter a final word of warning.

"Don't let your father talk you out of that dawn start," she said.

"Six on the dot," he promised. He caught her up and held her for a moment. "Darling, I love you. I'll be back in half an hour to tell you so in more detail."

He released her reluctantly and went away.

Gail paused at Mrs. Westerby's door, knocked and entered. Mrs. Westerby, a shawl over her dress, was seated on a low sofa before the open window. She said nothing, allowing Gail to take in the full beauty of the scene. The view was of a moonlit lake, mountains, wooded slopes. From here, the hotel was not visible; even the protective fencing was invisible in this light. The lake path could be seen at intervals between the trees and the water was no longer stirred by the breeze, but calm and still. Gail did not believe in ghosts, but she agreed with Mrs. Westerby, looking

out at the restful scene, that this was where ghosts might
walk—not restlessly, not seeking, but going over ground
they had known and loved in life.

"I never know quite how religious I am," she heard Mrs.
Westerby saying meditatively. "I can never quite reconcile
the simplicity of the first message with the hokey-pokey and
mumbo jumbo that came afterwards. It's only when I'm
here, at Chandon, that things fall into place. Everything
goes back to the beginning and I feel all right again. Do you
believe in anything? So many young people don't."

"I can do without what you called the hokey-pokey. I
thought I'd be a Catholic, once. They seemed to have no
problems—just swallowed it whole and took it in their
stride."

"But you changed your mind?"

"My brother changed my mind. He likes the idea of
marching up to God, eventually, and saying 'Well, here I
am, and I did my best—what's the score?' "

"I think I would like your brother."

"Everybody likes my brother. That's his trouble. Charm's
a terrible thing, for you don't have to worry about anything."

"Everything comes to you? Yes, I suppose so. And tomorrow you'll be with him, and I hope you'll forget us. That
is, I hope you will forget the things which have distressed
you on this journey."

It was difficult, listening to the quiet, level voice—which
for the first time she did not think ugly—for Gail to remember exactly what had distressed her. This large, likable
woman sitting so still, hands folded on her lap, her eyes
drinking in beauty—this woman had no possible connection

with the other—the loud-voiced, shambling creature from whom all who could escape, did so. The journey, she reflected, had kept everything good until the last.

"I shan't forget you," she said, "and it won't be long before you see me again."

She had an impulse to go on without pause and tell her what the future held—and then decided that Julian ought to break the news when he brought his father over from the hotel.

Mrs. Westerby took her hand and held it for a moment. "Goodbye—and thank you, my dear."

Gail bent and laid her lips on the soft cheek. Then she went out and closed the door quietly behind her.

She heard Mrs. Westerby going downstairs some time later. She heard her speaking to the old couple; all three went out together and Mrs. Westerby called up, from outside, to Gail's window.

"Julian seems to have gone for a stroll," she said, "and he forgot to take a key. The servants are going to their quarters, so I shall leave the key on this stone bench beside the front door. If Julian doesn't see it, will you call down to him?"

Gail promised that she would. She would not only call down; she would go down.

"I shall in all probability be back before him," Mrs. Westerby said. "I'm only going to sit for a little while in my favourite spot."

Gail stood watching the three figures as they moved away. The servants went to their rooms over the garage; Mrs. Westerby, swathed in her shawl, walked slowly up the grassy slope beyond the gardens, paused on the top and then went out of sight beyond the trees bordering the path. She could be seen again farther along, but only for a moment; then Gail knew she had almost reached the semicircular clearing that formed a kind of throne above the water.

She closed one-half of the window; it was chilly. She cleaned her teeth and finished the last of her packing and looked round the room to see that nothing was left out. Then she switched off the light and walked to the window and stood staring out. Yes, it was beautiful, she acknowledged. It was not even absurd, in this enveloping peace, to imagine Mrs. Westerby out there by the lake with the ghost of the gentle Edward. Perhaps she had already seen him; it would account for the serenity of her mood, for her calm, steady and strangely purposeful gait as she went towards the path by the lake.

Gail glanced at the sky. Now and then light clouds brushed across the moon, like someone passing a cloth over the surface to make it brighter. She yawned, and turned towards the light switch; she would read until she heard Julian coming back with his father.

And then she paused and slowly, unwillingly, turned to look out of the window once more.

Perhaps it was Julian, she told herself, but not hopefully. She knew well enough that it was not Julian. But until the figure came into view again, she would not know for certain. . . .

The figure reappeared, walking slowly, very slowly along the path. Now she knew for certain. It was Mrs. Stratton.

She ought to have known, Gail told herself with rising irritation, that this trip wasn't going to end on that pretty scene—soft light and gentle ghosts and a young girl's kiss on the withered cheek. How could she and Julian have been as naïve as to imagine that the disturbing events of the journey would close in an intimate dinner for two and a dawn departure? And what unlucky chance had directed her eyes to the sight of Mrs. Stratton coming to take a little walk beside the lake before going to bed? It would be easy, she knew, to pretend she had seen nothing. All she had to do, she told herself, dragging her coat roughly off its hanger, all she had to do—she kicked off her shoes and put on the moccasins she had put out for the morning—all she had to do was to take a running jump at the bed, pull the covers up to her chin, close her eyes and mind her own business and let Edward's ghost keep the two women from meeting one another.

For they must meet. She opened the door, switched on the landing light and went down the stairs. Mrs. Westerby was out there—serene and composed; but Mrs. Stratton was out there too, and Julian had stated specifically that no trouble would arise if the two women could be kept apart. This, after all, was the only thing she could do; go out and head Mrs. Stratton off before she reached the lookout and broke in on her sister-in-law's reverie.

For the change in the situation, the change from an atmosphere charged with tension to one of peace had come about simply because the two women had separated. The journey was over; one had gone to the hotel and the other had stayed in her cottage, and Julian's father was here to see to it that they did not meet again until the final discussion as to the disposal of the furniture. But nobody had expected this after-dinner wandering in the moonlight. Why couldn't people go to bed? Why did women, not in their first youth, take it into their heads to meander along narrow and—if the clouds grew thicker—dangerous paths looking for ghosts?

Edward's ghost. Which of them would consider she had first right to Edward's ghost? Mrs. Westerby. If he wanted to walk for his widow, she would argue, he wouldn't have chosen this place, where his widow had never before set foot and in which she was an interloper. If Edward was here, it would be because he had come home—to his own. It would be—

At this point, the clouds obscured the moon and Gail's fancies came to an abrupt end. She hesitated, and was preparing to go forward cautiously in the blackness towards the shimmer of water she could see through the trees, when to her relief the moon came out again and lighted her way.

She moved fast—she was not as near the path as she had thought and if she did not hurry she would not be in time to intercept Mrs. Stratton before she reached the belvedere. She tried to take the last of the slope at a run, only to find herself sliding down the slippery grass. She got up, and to her dismay caught a glimpse of Mrs. Stratton's dress as she passed behind the next line of trees.

For the first time since she had seen her from the window, Gail felt a stab of fear. It was one thing to intercept, to suggest turning and walking back to the hotel on this pleasant evening, or talking loudly to give Mrs. Westerby time to retreat if she wished to. But neither of these plans was now possible. If she wanted to keep the two women apart—and something told her it was vital that she should keep them apart—she would have to swerve to the left and come out among the trees to the left of the lookout.

She did not dare to call. Her heart was beating fast, and

her mouth was dry, and she wanted Julian so desperately
that she almost called his name aloud. She felt lost, lonely
and unqualified to cope with situations of this kind; she
felt that she had been trapped just when she was on the
point of escaping.

She grasped roots, branches, anything that held fast, and
pulled herself up the last steep yards. Then she was on level
ground. Through the trees she could see, ahead, the figure
of Mrs. Westerby standing motionless, gazing out over the
lake; behind her, not yet at the curve which would enable
her to see the older woman, Mrs. Stratton came with slow
steps.

Gail took a step forward—and then, without the slightest
warning, iron arms closed round her from behind. A hand
was clamped roughly over her mouth.

Terror rolled up and engulfed her. Her legs were free; she
kicked desperately, and then a trousered leg came round
and imprisoned hers, holding her helpless and immovable.
She could scarcely breathe; this was like drowning . . . like
strangling, she thought desperately.

And then she realized that she could see.

And she could hear. . . .

She could see, on either side of her, two men: motionless. One of them she recognized by his likeness to Julian;
it must be Julian, then, who held her in this paralyzing
grip. The two men were not looking at her; they were standing, grim and silent, watching Mrs. Westerby.

Gail did not know whether Mrs. Westerby had heard
Mrs. Stratton's approach; she did not think so, for the
ground was soft and even in this deathly stillness footsteps

were almost inaudible. But something must have made her
turn.

For seconds, nobody, nothing moved. Mrs. Stratton's
back was to the watchers, but as her eyes fell on the other
woman, Gail knew that she had never before seen so deep
a look of loathing on any face as on Mrs. Westerby's, who
was facing them.

She could not tell what Mrs. Stratton would do. If she
wished, she could turn and retreat by the way that she had
come—but Gail, who had ceased to struggle, ceased to think
of herself, knew that it would be like turning her back on
a loaded gun that was pointing towards her.

Mrs. Westerby spoke at last—a harsh, dragging voice.

"It was in this place," she said, "that I always wanted to
meet you. Here . . . with Edward." She paused. "I knew
you would come. I knew you had to come. Tonight, or tomorrow night, or any night. I knew you would come."

Mrs. Stratton said nothing; Gail thought that horror
would keep her silent; horror and fear of the naked hatred
in the face and the voice of the trembling old woman before
her.

And then Mrs. Westerby spoke again—three words which
sounded to Gail like an explosion shattering the night's
calm.

"You killed him."

The words seemed to echo and echo endlessly over the
mountains. Killed him . . . killed him . . . killed him. . . .

"Of course," Mrs. Stratton said quietly.

Gail's heart gave a lurch. The hand that bruised her
mouth was removed. Her legs were freed. The arms that

held her loosened. But she did not move—did not, could not utter a sound.

"I knew." Mrs. Westerby's words came between the rasping sounds made by her breathing. "I knew."

"You couldn't know," Mrs. Stratton corrected her, and her voice was still quiet, still gentle. "You could only guess, my dear Blanche."

"It was poison, wasn't it?"

"Yes."

"Dear, dear God. . . ." Mrs. Westerby spoke the words softly. "Yes, I knew, or I guessed. But I couldn't guess why. Why, why, why?"

"Money, Blanche, money." There was a softly mocking note in the soft tones. "Money—and the freedom to enjoy it. Not money to pour out, endlessly, keeping an invalid in the comfort in which you had always kept him. I had to look out for myself, you see. I wasn't going to be left a poor widow. Not a second time."

"The . . . the . . . your book," Mrs. Westerby brought out with difficulty. "You had money. . . ."

"The publishers took too long," Mrs. Stratton said with no change of tone. "If I had known earlier, perhaps it wouldn't have been necessary to . . . to go so far. But I think Edward would have been a little in the way, Blanche. As . . . as you are now."

Mrs. Westerby's face twisted.

"More poison?"

"Of course not." Mrs. Stratton spoke almost tenderly. "You have only to take two . . . perhaps three steps backwards."

"I would like to. Oh, I would like to," Mrs. Westerby said yearningly. "But that would leave you. . . ."

"Exactly. With everything of Edward's and . . . everything of yours. And I'm sure that Edward would like to know that you could no longer . . . interfere."

"I am stronger than you," Mrs. Westerby said. "You can't force me to move."

"No, that's true. But, you see, I came along this path earlier this evening and I . . . shall I show you? I moved this boulder. I have only to push it, and it will be quite, quite impossible for you to do anything but . . . join Edward."

And Gail, frozen with horror, saw that even as Mrs. Stratton spoke the name, the great stone had begun to move. What happened next, she was never afterwards to recall with any clarity; she was never afterwards to see clearly through the fog of terror that had obscured the scene. She knew that all three men had sprung forward. Julian's sudden movement sent her crashing against a tree, and she saw Mrs. Westerby caught and pinned against the stone. She saw, for a sickening instant, the face of bewilderment and fear that Mrs. Stratton turned on the three men. And she saw the look that supplanted the bewilderment and fear, the strange look of acceptance that Mrs. Stratton carried with her as she stepped backwards and reached blindly behind her for the support of the stone . . . the stone that had moved, that was no longer between her and the edge.

There was no cry as she fell, no scream. There were only the seconds of deathly waiting, and then the sound, scarcely a splash, that was heard as the body hit the water. The dry sobbing that succeeded the sound, Gail realized, when it had gone on for some time, came from herself. Julian's arms were round her; he was holding her as if he would never let her go, but even when the sobs ceased, her trembling continued.

From Mrs. Westerby, standing motionless on the edge and staring out across the water, there was no sound whatever.

Chapter Ten

"I KNEW," Mrs. Westerby said slowly. "I knew. I have known for a very long time."

"You didn't *know*." Julian's voice was gentle.

She gave him a brief, upward glance.

"I knew," she said again.

She paused, and they waited—Julian and his father, and Gail—in the quiet, dimly lighted drawing room. Outside, along the lake path, figures moved, voices sounded; tragedy had struck and a woman had fallen to her death, and the details were spreading with the rapidity of all such events. Two gentlemen, both of the police, though of different countries—England and France—had been walking together after dinner, and had witnessed her fall. What could be done, was being done, but Mrs. Westerby had been brought back to her cottage. There was nothing she could do. Nothing more.

"Yes, I knew." Her tone was firmer. "You're trying to tell me that I guessed, or surmised, or felt that something was terribly wrong. I can only say that I *knew*—and my knowledge wasn't based on anything but plain, clear facts. The facts wouldn't have meant much to anybody but myself, but I could read them clearly enough, and they all pointed to something which I was afraid to look at. My mind, my brain told me what was going on, but I couldn't, I wouldn't accept it. It was too horrible, too terrible . . . even to myself, right up to the end, there was always one piece missing. Why? Day and night, I asked myself that question: Why?" She beat with a clenched fist repeatedly on the palm of her hand. "Why, why, why? Why marry him? If money was her object, why not try for a much richer man? And why wait so long before deciding to . . . to do away with him?

"When I first began to realize, there was nobody to whom I could go—except Julian's father. He knew me. We had known one another for more than forty years. I felt that he was the only person in the world who would listen to me without fearing that my grief had upset the balance of my mind. But I could hear, as I tried to talk to him the first time, how unlikely, how melodramatic my words sounded. And the greatest horror of all was reading in his eyes the knowledge that when you become an old woman and have a reputation for eccentricity, even your best and oldest friends are prepared to believe that perhaps you've grown more than eccentric, that you're becoming just a little crazy. I could sense, when he spoke, the worry behind his words."

"He was worried," Julian said, "because he believed you."

"Right to the end, he couldn't really bring himself to believe that somebody so close to Edward, to me, could prove . . . could prove so diabolically clever, could. . . ."

She stopped; she was breathing with difficulty. Julian's father asked her if she would like to rest, and she shook her head.

"Let me talk," she begged. "Let me talk, at last, to people who know that what I'm saying is not the raving of a senile old woman. Let me talk. Let me tell you all, telling it all as clearly as I can, not keeping back anything in the fear of overtaxing your belief, of being warned about hysteria, of—"

"I just asked you to rest," Julian's father said mildly. "Never for one moment, Blanche, did I ever really doubt—"

"No." She studied him for a few moments. "No, Walter, I don't think you did. I should have remembered that you saw her, met her, perhaps measured her from the beginning better than I could. In the beginning, I was so eager to like her, to be liked by her. Edward's marriage was perhaps a surprise, a shock, but when he brought her to see me, I couldn't help seeing what had attracted him. I applauded his taste. She was so pretty, so quiet, so good to him . . . I was grateful to her. All I hoped was that I could now and then see them, odd and peculiar though she might think me.

"But I saw, almost at once, that I was to be kept away. The move down to Cornwall was surely made to get away from me—to get Edward away from me. I thought it was pure coincidence—and his wife's illness—that took old Dr. Belldon down there, but of course it was her—Anita's—doing."

"Are you saying," Julian asked, "that even then she was planning to—"

"Kill him? I think so. She had married once before, but she hadn't been able to get control of her husband's money. He—or he and she together—spent it. When she married for the second time, she was determined to see that she was not left again with nothing.

"She had never met me, but Edward must have told her

a good deal. I lived in the family home. I had most of the family possessions. Edward had a comfortable income, but my husband had left me a much larger one, and at my death, it would go to Edward. She must have longed to kill me—but she must have guessed that I would be hard to kill. So she remembered that I was old, and perhaps she would not have long to wait. . . .

"And then she realized that Edward's delicate constitution was a fact, and not my fancy. It was not fuss, engendered by living with a cossetting sister; he was, in fact, a man who would have to have constant care. And when she knew that, she grew frightened. She began to plan. Not to kill him, perhaps. Not then. She merely planned to get every penny he possessed into her own name. And so began the story of financial difficulties. So began the fiction of having to sell, and sell, to meet the expenses of constant illness. And I began to see that something was wrong, because when I paid them a visit at that time, I saw that she had begun to sell things of value."

"The miniatures?" Gail spoke for the first time.

"No, not the miniatures. Not then. They were sold later —and in a way that told me that what until then I scarcely dared to put into words, was true.

"They were beautiful, and very valuable. When she put them on the market, she took them, as she had taken other things, to an antique dealer. He happened to know me. He had thought nothing of the other sales—a pretty woman making a little money to cover this or that extravagance. But the miniatures were different. They were family things. They were painted of and for my family, and one of them was the pair to one in my own possession. She had asked him to sell them privately and quietly, but he felt so strongly about the matter that, privately and quietly, he came to me to suggest that I might care to become the private, quiet buyer.

"I bought them. I have them today. I paid a magnificent price for them, first because they were worth it, and next because I saw a way of proving, for the first time, what I had only suspected before. I bought them at a very high figure—and after a time, I paid a visit to Cornwall."

There was a long silence. Mrs. Westerby was staring into the past, and they did not disturb her.

"She said nothing whatsoever about the sale of the miniatures," she went on slowly. "She told me nothing of any sales. She just told me that she was nursing Edward day and night, and that he was losing ground.

"I asked her about money. There was not much, she said, but she and Edward preferred to manage on what there was; even if she could bring herself to accept money from me, she told me, it would be impossible to persuade Edward to agree.

"And so much was true. When she took me in to see Edward, I read death on his face—but she sat beside him and held his hand, and spoke gently—oh, so gently—and smiled and explained that Blanche was anxious to help but they had decided—hadn't they?—that being poor had no terrors for them. She said that being poor had—hadn't it?—brought them closer to one another. She said most of it; all poor Edward added was that he wanted nothing for himself, only for Anita—and if Anita felt happier managing to make ends meet without help, even from me—there was no way of persuading her. Everything she said was agreed to or corroborated by him. He watched her with affection and with gratitude and with a sort of wonder that she should do so much, so uncomplainingly, for him."

Once more Mrs. Westerby stopped.

"When she had all the money," she went on quietly after a time, "she had nothing more to wait for. But one thing delayed her. She had written a book.

"The doctor said that putting it in the hands of the publishers was entirely his own doing, but if he had been questioned closely, I think it would have been found that she had given him the book and suggested the visit to London at the right moment.

"The book was put into Christopher Beetham's hands. And Anita waited. She had money, but not money she could use immediately after Edward's death. She could not fall back on the fiction of his life insurance. A man as delicate as he had always been would have had difficulty in arranging a policy that brought in a very large sum. But if the book was accepted, she could, whether it met with small or great success, ascribe her sudden change of fortune to her writing. She had only to wait, and hope.

"But no word came. She must have known that the book had power, but she could not guess how it would strike a reader. She waited, and no word came, and so she decided she would wait no longer. And so . . . Edward died. Edward died. Edward . . . died. . . ."

Julian's father put a hand on her shoulder.

"No more, Blanche," he said. "You must—"

"Forget?"

"You must stop talking about it until—"

"Until I can talk without feeling? Let me go on, Walter."

He removed his hand, but did not move from her side.

"I knew," she said, "when I heard of his death, that she had had a hand in it. But what could I hope to prove? How could I even hope to get a hearing from anybody? I could prove her a cheat and a liar, but beyond that, who would listen to me? Nobody. Dr. Belldon was an innocent accomplice. The cause of death was not a matter that had ever raised any questions. I was a jealous and possessive old woman and I had loved my brother and his death had sent me a little off my head—that would have been the reaction, at its kindest. If I spoke, I labelled myself unbalanced—and there was still the small, faint chance, the small, faint hope that I was mistaken.

"And then . . . I read her book.

"It was not written by a woman looking backwards. It was written by a woman looking into the future. The waste, the desert, wasn't behind her, but before her . . . if she let herself accept life as it offered itself. Life with a sick man, life on a moderate income, or—even if there was money enough for the luxury she loved—the sick man still to care for. She was not looking back. She was looking forward to life as it might be—if she did not take her fate into her own hands. Every line in the book was her portrayal of her life and what it could become—if she let it. From each one of the failures she described in the book—lack of money, lack of opportunity, lack of friends, of luxury, of travel—from each one of these she was determined to save herself. She had once married for money—and the money had evaporated. She had chosen a second man with money—and had discovered that she had an invalid on her hands. She put down in her book her alternative to killing—a life spent in taking what fate handed out, without attempting to fight back.

"I read the book, and then I was sure she had killed Edward. And I went to Julian's father, and for the first time I heard myself saying, aloud, the terrible things I had suspected for so long. And he looked at me with fear in his eyes."

"Could you have expected me," asked Walter Meredith, "to hear what you said—and not be afraid?"

"You were afraid to believe me."

"I didn't dare to disbelieve you. But to a man like myself, a man of my profession, you had to bring more proof than could be read between the lines of a book. When you spoke of cheating and lying, I knew that you could produce proof —but murder?"

The word was spoken for the first time. It seemed to bring into the room all the horror of the past few hours. His face white, Julian stared at his father.

"It was no less terrible to imagine it then, than to know it now," Walter said. "I was frightened—for Blanche. She had no proof, and no hope of finding any. Everything would operate against her if she tried to bring her suspicions into the open. I feared the effect she would have on any member of the police—if she went to the police. I knew her and I could vouch for her intelligence and her sanity—but I could visualize their reactions when she put her suspicions before them—"

"And saw the object of them," Mrs. Westerby ended quietly. "That was the fact, above all others, that steadied me, that kept me from speaking to anybody but Walter. How could I hope to convince? How could I hope to sustain any accusation against her? I was old and odd. She was the very picture of womanly goodness and dutifulness and graciousness. What chance had I?

"Only one." She looked at Gail. "Only one—and Julian's father will tell you how little, how very little, we trusted in its success.

"I agreed to meet her at Chandon. And after that, all I hoped for was to trap her into self-betrayal. I knew that I could work on a side of her that was vulnerable—her hatred of me. I had, once or twice, by my blunderings, got past her guard. Once or twice, in the house in Cornwall, distress and a feeling of helplessness had perhaps made me go too far, had made me try to interfere too much, and I had seen the mask slip. It seemed to me that if only someone else could be there as witness—if only someone of undisputed authority, like Walter, could see for himself that she had another, a darker, a more dangerous side—they would believe the evil I imputed to her. I was no detective. I had no clues, no hope of finding any. I was helpless to act—except in this way. I could irritate her. I could anger her. I had irritated and angered her, in the past, to the point . . . almost to the point of making her lose her self-control. I wondered if I could do it again. I wondered if, given circumstances in which I could goad her, even perhaps humiliate her before others, I might crack the mask, destroy the smooth, smiling façade.

"But Walter decided not to come with me."

"For many reasons," Walter Meredith said, "the chief of which was that I was afraid of meeting someone who knew me in my official capacity. Any word of police or detectives would be enough to put her on her guard—even

perhaps to warn her. I decided to ask Julian to come out
with Blanche. He was as fond of her, he trusted her as much
as I myself did. He would keep an eye on her if trouble developed—and we feared it would. Blanche hoped that opportunities might occur—"

"I didn't hope, Walter—I knew. I knew that if I could
find out when her plane was due, I could arrange for Julian
and myself to be somewhere we could follow, or wait for
Gail's car. There would be no difficulty in that. The only
difficulty would be getting at her when other people were
present to watch us, to laugh at us. When I knew that Sir
Hugo had travelled out with her, had shown enough interest
in her to book a room for himself at the hotel here, I
thanked God."

"What really happened at that café on the roadside,
Blanche?" Julian asked.

She sighed. "I think perhaps I was a little mad," she said.
"I knew Gail's car could not be far behind, as I had given
her details of the route she was to follow. I was hoping to
delay so that she could catch us up. I had no more definite
plan than to watch the road from the terrace and, with
every appearance of surprise, hail Gail's car as it passed.
With anyone else beside her, Anita would have gone on.
With Gail driving, I knew the car would stop. And so I
left Julian and I walked towards the road. . . .

"And then I saw the workmen, and the arrow, and the
notice. And again, I saw the hand of God. I dropped my
scarf round the notice and I turned the arrow round to point
in the wrong direction. I saw Gail's car, I saw the big car
with the Americans, the small car with the Germans . . .
and then Julian came towards me, and behind him were

some workmen, and I knew that we had to get away at once, because the men would realize that something was wrong, and put it right again. So I hurried Julian to the car, and when he protested that the bypass was leading us nowhere, I told him that I knew the district and that we should shortly find ourselves on the main road again.

"And so we stayed at the inn, and I said one more fervent prayer—that I would be able to goad Anita and drive her out of her corner and expose her to the kind of attention she could least bear—ridicule. She couldn't get away. We were linked together by our relationship to Edward. She couldn't escape, couldn't detach herself, couldn't repudiate me. I was a sight, a show, an intolerable nuisance to everybody, a laughing stock, a hideous embarrassment to her. And when at last I mentioned the miniatures, she could not fail to see that I was also a threat to everything she had taken so much trouble to plan, gone to so much risk to obtain. Before we left the inn—and certainly when Sir Hugo left the inn, driven away by me—I think she had begun to dream of disposing of me. And then . . . I showed her how it could be accomplished with speed and safety. And so I led you all to the lake. . . ."

They could see it, calm and shimmering and deadly. They could see it, and they could see once again a slim body falling. . . .

"You all think," came Mrs. Westerby's slow, dragging voice, "you all think I wanted revenge. I didn't want revenge. Edward died by her hand—a long, drawn-out and terrible death. But revenge, I've always believed, is a kind of poison in itself. What would revenge have done for Edward? It wouldn't bring him back. All I wanted was proof of her guilt. It sounds incredible now, but I think if she had confessed, on the lake path, what she had done, how she had done it, why she had done it . . . then I would have been at peace. I know that what I'm saying is stupid. Crime is crime, and has to be punished—but I would like you to believe that from first to last I wasn't thinking in terms of crime and punishment. What was she to me? My only thought was of my brother. He had died, and I was sure she had murdered him, and I was haunted by the feeling that even if he had loved her, even if he wanted her to go unpunished, it was terrible to leave him forever without doing anything to discover the truth about his death."

"Perhaps he did know the truth about his death," Walter suggested quietly.

"No." She swung round and spoke with utter conviction. "No. He knew nothing. You must remember that illness, for him, was almost a habit. He suspected nothing. I was the only one who suspected anything—too late to help him. As I saw it, I was bound to bring the truth to light—if I could. Not for revenge—just for the sake of truth. He died with only a lying, murderous woman at his side. He wouldn't have wanted revenge, but I think he would have been glad to know that Walter and I had followed him beyond the grave, had cared enough to . . . I can only tell you that now, for the first time since his death, I seem to be close to him. But I swear that I had no thought beyond the proving of my suspicions. I wanted her guilt established. That, for me, was to have been the end. I never once looked beyond."

She sat unmoving, her hands held loosely on her lap. She looked to Gail like a statue of age in defeat—age stripped of its last shreds of beauty or wisdom or vigour, and exposed in all its weakness and ugliness.

She felt Mrs. Westerby take one of her hands and hold it.

"You must go tomorrow, as you planned, Gail," she said. "Early in the morning—you and Julian. You have told me nothing, but I know that he will never leave you again. This is no place for either of you. I am sorry that you saw so much. You will have to forgive me. I could have prevented your coming. Julian knows that I could have stopped you—but I didn't want to. When I heard that it was in your car that Anita was coming here, I felt that I must meet you, see you, if possible give you a little glimpse of myself and my home. I wanted to have you . . . I don't say on my side, because I didn't think of it in those terms. I was afraid of what you might hear about me from Anita. She wouldn't, I knew, say anything definite, but she could have made you see me as a woman eccentric to the point of madness—a woman to be feared. I thought that if you met me, saw me in my own setting, realized that I was living a quiet and perhaps useful life, with friends round me who respected me, you would remember. Later on, you might have the picture distorted a little, but you seemed to me intelligent enough, steady enough, balanced enough to preserve some kind of respect for me. And, thank God, you did. For I am certain that, but for you, she would have changed her mind about going to the cottage. I had mentioned the miniatures, and frightened her. She had two choices—to go back, or to go on. You made her go on."

Gail released the thick, flabby hand. Yes, she had made Mrs. Stratton go on—and she had gone to her death. There had been a choice, and it had been left to her to make the final, the fatal decision. She had told Julian that all this was nothing to do with her, and she thought that she had spoken the truth, but now she could see that her involvement began on the day of the reception given by the Beetham Brothers on the terrace of the Courtier Restaurant.

She saw the two men assisting Mrs. Westerby to rise. She opened the door and watched them as they went into the hall and up the stairs. Then she turned slowly back to the quiet room and stared out at the gleaming water, waiting for Julian. Out there Anita Stratton had died—because she had not been permitted to run away. She had been persuaded to go on—to the end.

Chapter Eleven

THEY had left the mountains behind. Before them was the coast, and every kilometer was bringing them nearer to the heavy traffic and the tourists.

Julian was driving Tim Sinclair's car; his own would be driven back to England by his father—and Mrs. Westerby would go with him. Julian's immediate objective was to restore the car he was driving to its owner; he did not propose to give up his passenger too.

"But he'll expect me to go back with him," Gail pointed out.

"Do you want to?"

"Not without you, naturally—but suppose he's got—"

"Let's suppose nothing until we see him," Julian suggested.

"And we tell him nothing?"

"Not yet. Perhaps not at all. What, after all, has it got to do with anybody but the people directly involved? It's finished. You can tell your family as much or as little as you want to, but if you decide to tell them, I'd wait a few months." He paused. "It's going to be hard for you, going back to the Beetham Brothers."

"Do I have to?"

"Yes, you have to. But not for long."

The Stratton file, she thought. It would not be closed. The money would still pour in, the book would still sell. But there would be no more lunches with Mr. Thomas, no more receptions. No more interviews. Miss Teller would marvel at her own psychic powers; she had sensed, she would say, that something was going to happen. . . .

"Promise not to brood," she heard Julian saying.

"I promise. Do we tell Tim straight off that we're going to get married? Couldn't we give him the impression that we'd known each other for . . . well, for longer than we have?"

"Let him ask the questions first. Then we'll think of the answers. Does he look anything like you?"

"No. More like Noelle."

Julian, however, found that there was very little likeness in Tim to either sister. All he recognized was Gail's directness of speech.

It took some time to locate him. They began at the hotel, went on to a house in which, they were told, he was visiting friends. The friends had just left; yes, an Englishman had left with them.

"Scotsman," Gail said, as they drove to the next clue. "Why can't people differentiate?"

"He mustn't have been wearing his tam-o'-shanter. Where's this restaurant?"

"Second on the left."

He was not there. They went back to the hotel and found that he had returned. Would they go up to his room?

He yelled from the bathroom, and a few minutes later,

emerged draped, Roman-fashion, in a large towel. He kissed his sister, shook hands with Julian and asked what the holdup had been.

"I said I'd drive somebody to a place—"

"Car going well?" he enquired anxiously.

"The car's all right. Julian drove it from Chandon to here."

"Chandon? Oh, this place you were talking about. Women," he explained to Julian, "think that cars can run indefinitely without servicing. A girl in Malta actually wrecked the engine of a beautiful job—and when it was towed to the garage, 'Oil?' said she, all wide-eyed, 'Oh, I for-got!'— You mean you came here in my car with Gail?"

"Yes."

"Where did you meet? At this place—what's it called?— Chandon?"

"No, we met in England and then we met again out here," Gail said. "You'd better take a good look. He's coming into the family."

"No!" Surprise made the bath towel slip, and Tim clutched it. "What—really? Mrs. Julian Meredith, and all that?"

"Yes."

"Blow me down," Tim said simply. "Well, congratulations. Nobody breathed a word."

"Nobody had a word to breathe. You're the first—nearly—to know."

"Bless you, my children. I must say this makes things rather easier for me. I had a little problem."

"A girl?" guessed Gail.

Tim hesitated. Then a happy smile spread over his face.

"Well, in a manner of speaking, yes," he said. "A female. Very beautiful, very expensive. She's flying to England today."

"And you want to go with her. And you didn't know what to do with Gail—is that it?" Julian asked.

"Correct."

"What's her name?" Gail asked.

"It's . . . well, it's an odd name. I first saw her down in the south, about eighteen months ago. I fell in love with her, but I couldn't do much about it then. I fixed it so's she'd be here to meet me—and she's flying home at four-thirty, which means a pretty swift move for all of us, if you want to come and see us off."

"English?" Gail asked.

"Good Lord, no. She . . . well, she's got a lot of Arab blood."

"She's not a girl," Julian said. "You've bought a horse."

"A magnificent beast," Tim said with a rapt expression. "I was staying with these Spanish people, and I went riding with them—they knew I was keen on riding, but until that morning, I'd never—Gail will vouch for this—never had the slightest interest in anything else to do with horses. But it was like being on the flying trapeze. . . . And now she's mine, and what I'd like you to do, Gail"—he dropped the towel absentmindedly and reached for a shirt—"is get on the phone to Alan when you've seen me off, and tell him I'd like to keep her at the farm and—"

"It isn't Alan you need," Gail said. "I'll get through to Lydia, his sister."

"What for?"

"Because she knows more about horses than you're likely

to pick up for years. She'll stable it and she'll look after it, while you're on leave and when you've gone away again. Lydia's the one you want."

"You'll explain, won't you, that this animal is something rather special?"

"Yes."

"Thanks. Did I give you two my blessing, incidentally? If not, take it as read. Is the car downstairs?"

"Yes," Julian said. "When we've taken you to the airport, do we—"

"Then you simply go on as you've been going—only in the opposite direction. I'll see you at the farm. In a way, it's silly to drag out to the airport—why don't you just put me in that coach affair? We'll make it if we go now. Go down and pay my bill, Gail, will you? Step on it."

He drove away in the airline coach, already looking, Gail commented, like a horse.

"That's that," she said. "You've met my family—all except my grandmother. Now I'm going to telephone to Noelle."

"Noelle? I thought you were going to get hold of that girl—what was her name?"

"Lydia. Noelle will fix it." She slipped her hand into Julian's. "Isn't it like an answer to prayer?"

"What is?"

"Well, Tim and Lydia."

"What about them?"

"Well, isn't it obvious?"

"Not to me. She's going to look after his horse, or so I gathered. What else did you have in mind?"

She began to tell him, and then decided not to. The

farm was a long way away; they would get to it in time. For the moment, she and Julian were alone, far from home and family—and with an open road before them.

"Julian—" she said.

"Well?"

She wanted to say that she loved him, but they were not as alone as all that, she remembered.

"Nothing," she said. "Let's go."

About the Author

Born and brought up in India, ELIZABETH CADELL was educated in Calcutta, London and Darjeeling. The early death of her husband left her with two small children to support, and after working at various secretarial positions, she decided to try writing. Her decision resulted in *Last Straw for Harriet*, Mrs. Cadell's first novel, published in 1947. Since then she has written over twenty books and her deft, light-hearted novels have been compared to those of Margery Sharp, Nancy Mitford, Angela Thirkell and P. G. Wodehouse. She recently settled in Portugal but remains true to her resolution "not to let the possession of a house keep me from going away from it." In the past few years she has traveled throughout Europe and in North America.